GIRLS JUST WANNA HAVE FUND$ 2

BRIANN DANAE

GIRLS JUST WANNA HAVE FUNDS 2

by BriAnn Danae

To my readers, thanks for your patience. This is book #42 and dedicated to you.

Bianca, Sequaia & Dominique... thank God for blessing me with you three. Your presence and friendship was **(and has always been)** truly appreciated while writing this book. I love y'all!

SYNOPSIS

In utter outrage, Zari lashes out at her so-called father, Zeek. Confusion racked her brain as to why he decided to pop back into her life. Amid her turmoil with Zeek and Maverick, Flip is fed up with being put to the side. Not knowing a thing about how to truly love a man, Zari finds herself about to lose him and the only piece of normalcy in her chaotic life.

Dismayed at the news of her son being in the hospital, Envie regrets going against her morals to set Urban up. She began to realize that he's much more than a handsome face and deep pockets. As their relationship blossoms, the guard she had up slowly dissolved. The once uninterested single mother is smitten by his charm and hopes her past doesn't ruin the chances of encountering real love.

The scandalous situation Misani is put in has caused a

strain between her and Carlo. All she ever wanted to do was provide a life worth living for her people without the struggle and heartache. Placing her emotions on the back-burner, she bosses up like always and takes one for the team; her girls. But will her decision cost her the life she's established or is Carlo and Xander willing to give her another chance?

On a quest to save her mother, Keegan is taught a harsh lesson about addiction. It's not something that can change overnight, though she wishes it could. With Ramzi in her corner every step of the way, he provides a shield that helps mend her broken heart. Can he keep saving her from her demons, or will Keegan finally come to terms with life being the way it is?

While money was the motive and at the top of each girl's agenda before, life quickly rearranged their priorities. In this final installment, lives are threatened, relationships are placed on trial, and the mission to find love and funds is more complicated than they bargained for.

CHAPTER ONE

B reathing heavily into the carpet, Zari's eyes burned with every ounce of hatred in her body. Not only was she pissed off for Maverick punching her like she was some man on the street, but her absentee father, Zeek, had the nerve to pop up on the scene. Lighting him up with her taser didn't give her the triumphant gratification she thought it would.

"Aye!" Urban yelled out. "Y'all don't have to be that rough with her."

"That bitch stole my chain, bro!" Maverick seethed.

"And she ain't leaving up out of here until he gets it back," his fiancée had the nerve to yell out – looking dumber than she already was looking and feeling.

Coming to, Zeek stood to his feet with the help from other officers. The second he was down, Zari was hoping she'd shocked his ass into cardiac arrest. Sadly, that didn't happen. Glaring at him with her arms behind her back, her nostrils flared in disgust. He looked as pitiful as he should've felt.

"You alright?" Zeek's partner questioned.

"I'm fine," he grumbled, a bit shook up and caught completely off guard.

Staring at the mug on Zari's face, he shook his head. "Let her go."

"But, she assaulted you."

Zeek stepped closer toward them. "I said, let her go. I got her."

"No," Zari hissed. "You need to be worried about that nigga! You saw him punch me!"

"And I'ma handle that if you chill out," Zeek spoke evenly.

He reached out to grab her arm, forcing Zari to snatch away from him. She didn't want his deadbeat ass anywhere near her.

"Are we taking him downtown?" Zeek's partner questioned, referring to Maverick.

"Give me a second," he said before nodding his head toward the other end of the hall. "Let me speak to you over here."

"We don't have shit to discuss. I can promise you that," Zari spoke harshly.

Her chest heaved with animosity and revenge. The blow Maverick delivered had her jaw tender and her anger at an all-time high. What pissed her off, even more, was knowing she couldn't get this nigga touched because he was a celebrity. Had she been able to, Zari was calling up Jhalil and all her male cousins. Since she couldn't she was going to get payback another way. A way only she knew how.

Sighing, Zeek pleaded with her to speak with him. "Look, I'm trying to make sure they don't haul your ass to jail."

Stubbornly, she inched down the opposite side of the hall and crossed her arms. "What?"

"What's going on? Did you steal from him?"

Zari scoffed. "As if that should matter. He put his hands on me, and if you don't cuff his ass and take him downtown, I'm airing your business out."

A flash of alarm settled in Zeek's eyes. "Are you serious right now?"

"Does it look like I'm playing?" Zari spat back.

Zeek groaned and gritted his teeth. "This shit has nothing to do with my past."

Zari shrugged. "Yeah, well, I don't give a fuck. You suddenly want to protect and serve but pimped women out including my mother, so I don't care. Have his ass arrested or else," she threatened meaning every word.

Going over the options in his head, Zeek knew he didn't have many. But, he had an ultimatum. He always did.

"The only way I'm taking him downtown is if you agree to meet with me sometime next week. We need to talk."

Going into his pocket, Zeek pulled out one of his business cards and held it out for her to grab. Zari stared at his outreached hand in disgust but knew what she had to do. Snatching the card up, she shoved it in her back pocket.

"So, we have a deal?" Zeek questioned, eyes full of hope.

"For now. I'll be down at the station to press charges in the morning, and you better have records of his ass being there."

Zeek sighed and watched as Zari walked away. He was only steps behind her before telling his partner to cuff Maverick and have him taken downtown.

"Are you serious right now!" Maverick shouted, cutting his eyes Zari's way. "Bitch, you gon' see me!"

"Yeah, see me in court. You put your hands on the wrong one, honey," Zari smirked, but her facial expression quickly fell when Urban grabbed her by the elbow. She frowned looking at Envie. "What's wrong?"

"We gotta get to the hospital. Her son was just rushed there."

Zari gasped and took quick steps toward Envie. "What's wrong with Azai?"

Envie's voice trembled as she answered, "I-I don't know."

Tears filled her eyes, and before Zari let these bitches see her friend break down, she turned her away from them and headed toward the elevator. Urban's security had already alerted his driver to meet them downstairs. Inside the elevator, Zari rubbed Envie's back soothingly, letting nothing but positive words flow from her lips. Even in her pissed off state, her friend needed her.

Urban looked on as Envie held her composure the best she could. She was afraid of the unknown, and the alarm in her sister, Elise's, voice didn't make the situation any better. From having his own child, Urban knew the lengths he'd go and had gone to protect his son from harm, and he had no doubt Envie had done and would do the same. The passion in her voice when Azai was brought up let him know that much.

"My driver is out front," he let them know as they exited the elevator.

Rushing outside, his driver greeted them right out front. He held the backdoor of the Navigator open as Zari climbed in first, with Envie and Urban right behind her.

"I need you to break every speed limit there is Deuce," Urban told him.

"Got you, boss."

Grabbing ahold of Envie's trembling hand, Urban caressed it and pulled her closer to him. She blinked rapidly, trying to keep her tears at bay. She didn't want to cry in front of him, but damn was it a struggle not to. Azai was her baby. Her heart in human form. Though she tried not to think the worst, Envie couldn't help but to.

"He gon' be good. His name doesn't mean strength for nothing," Urban spoke lowly into her ear.

Envie sniffled and held his hand tighter. She had to believe that if nothing else, Azai was going to fight. He'd been a fighter all his life. Closing her eyes, she called on God to cover her child in his time of need. She asked him to cover her as well. The reason for his hospital visit was unknown, and she hoped she didn't spazz out once she arrived.

Deuce followed Urban's instructions and had them at the hospital in fifteen minutes. He didn't bother to find a parking spot; just let them out at the door. Rushing inside, Envie placed her feelings to the side and got in warrior mommy mode. After the front desk receptionist let her know which floor Azai was on, they shuffled onto yet another elevator. Envie's hands were shaking, breathing labored, and eyes misty the higher the elevator climbed. At the sound of the ding, she hustled out with Urban, his security, and Zari right behind her.

Before she could make it to the nurse's station, the group of people sitting in the waiting area caused her brows to dip in confusion. In an instant, her mood went from saddened to angry.

"What're you doing here?" she damn near growled.

Misha, Zaire's first baby mama, sat in one of the chairs with her son and sister by her side.

"The same reason you're here," she sighed. "I had to rush Azai here."

"I'm sorry, what?" Envie questioned, knowing she couldn't have heard her correctly. "Why'd you have to rush him here? Where's Elise?"

"She's back there with Azai."

Envie's lips tightened as she let out a deep breath through her nose. "Okay... that's still not telling me what you're here for? I dropped Azai off with my sister before I left."

"And your mama dropped him off with me," Misha shot back, getting annoyed with Envie's tone. "He fell off the bottom bunk while he was asleep, and here we are."

"He fell off the bottom bunk?" Envie questioned lowly, not believing one word her ass was saying.

Misha couldn't stand Envie, and she had made it very clear from the first day she found out about her. Zaire had been open about them dating and even when he'd gotten her pregnant. The thing was, Misha knew all about Envie while Envie had no clue about her. Not until after she found out she was pregnant. The hate Misha held for Envie was sickening. The love she wanted Zaire to continuously show and give her all stopped when she came into the picture. Now, with him being locked up, her hatred for Envie hadn't disappeared at all.

"You sure somebody didn't push him off? He's too young to be sleeping on a bunk bed in the first place," Zari questioned, ready to snatch her ass up.

"Girl didn't nobody push your son. Questioning me like I'm lying. You should've had your son at home and not had him dropped off with me," Misha shrugged.

"Bitch," Envie damn near growled, stepping closer to her. She was about to go upside her head had Urban not pulled her back.

"Nah," he spoke into her ear, holding her around the waist. "Not here. Let's check on little man first."

Envie ice grilled Misha and the smirk she had on her face. It was as if Azai being hurt brought her joy. She was a sick individual for sure.

"You know what," Zari scoffed before saying, "You a bum ass bitch. On everything. You up here smirking because her son is hurt? Had it been yours, you'd be on a rampage."

"See, that's the difference between me and her. It'd never be my son cause I'm not leaving him with nobody I don't trust. Don't blame me for what happened, blame her bum ass mama and sister for not watching after him."

Before she even knew what happened, Zari punched the shit out of her. "Youse a stupid ass broad!"

Misha's sister tried getting buck, but Urban's security guard held her back. When Misha rushed to stand up, he grabbed ahold of her too. They weren't about to get anywhere near Urban.

"Let me go!" Misha yelled, just as Elise rounded the corner.

"Aye! What's going on?"

"You tell me," Envie grilled her. "Why was my son at her house when I left him with you?"

The anger in Envie's eyes had Elise spooked. She hadn't seen that side of her sister in a while. Envie was the peaceful one, but when it came to Azai, she'd turn up on anyone, anywhere. Family or not. The fact that she'd trusted her sister to watch after her son only for him to end up in the hands of a bitch who hated her guts had Envie ready to fight her own blood. Elise needed to start explaining and quickly.

"I'm going to need you guys to quiet down, or I'll have to call security," a nurse walked over and told them.

"No need," Misha spat. "We're leaving anyway. Let's go, Zaire." She smirked, loving the fact that her son had his daddy's name.

His security made sure nothing else popped off as he guided them to the elevators under Urban's instruction. Zari mugged them until the doors closed and promised to have her cousins run down on her before the week was up. For hers, Misha wasn't going to get by with none of that slick shit she was popping off. Especially not when it came to her nephew.

"Don't just stand there!" Envie shouted, making Elise flinch. "Start talking."

"Can we wait? Azai is back there with the doctor, and I just came to see if you were here."

Envie clenched her jaw. "Let's go."

"I'ma wait out here for you," Urban told her, taking a seat.

Envie's eyes softened when she faced him. "You sure? I don't know how long we're going to be here."

Urban nodded and gave her a reassuring smile. "I'm sure. Check on little man. I'll be here if you need me."

Sheepishly, Envie gave him a smile and nodded before heading down the hall with Zari by her side.

Elise led them to the room Azai was in, and Envie swallowed back her tears seeing her baby laid up in the bed. Thankfully, he was asleep because Envie did not need him seeing her break down. Wrapping him in her arms as best as she could without waking him, she held him and placed kisses across his caramel face. He looked so peaceful, but Envie could only imagine the pain he was in.

Everyone stood silently around the room watching their interaction. Elise held her own tears back, knowing her nephew wouldn't even be here had it not been for her selfishness. Running a hand over his forehead, Envie kissed him there and breathed a sigh of relief.

"What did the doctor say?" she asked Elise.

"He has a broken arm from the fall. They gave him some pain medicine, and he fell right to sleep. They'll be back to put a cast on his arm now that you're here."

Envie's jaw ticked. "Why the fuck was he at Misha's house?"

"I don't know," Elise whined. "I dropped him off with mama because Mase wanted to take me out. I didn't know she was going to drop him off over there. She told me she'd watch him until I got back."

"So you had mama watch Azai so you could go and get fucked by some nigga who doesn't care about you? You know how she feels about me and Azai, so why would you think that's cool?" Envie's voice trembled.

The way Lenae showed favoritism between her daughters hadn't changed over the years. In fact, it'd gotten worse. Especially when she realized Envie didn't need her for shit anymore. The only reason she'd stayed living under her roof for as long as she had was because of

Elise and her niece Emry. Lenae was jealous of her daughter and had been for years. She blamed Envie for Elise popping up pregnant and talked so bad to her when she found out she was pregnant with Azai. Envie had no clue why Lenae treated her the way that she did, and she long ago stopped trying to make amends. For her peace of mind she'd learned to handle her mother from a distance at a young age.

"I'm sorry. I didn't know she'd drop him off over there. I wasn't even planning to be gone that long. I promise."

"That's not the point. My baby is laid up with a broken arm because you wanted to go out and be fast."

"It wasn't like that! Don't act like I deliberately left him with mama knowing she'd do some shady shit like that. I'm not the one to blame," Elise said emotionally, with tears pooling in her eyes.

Squeezing her eyes shut, Envie took a few deep breaths. She had to calm her nerves. It was bad enough she couldn't beat Misha's ass, and now she was taking her frustrations out on her sister. She knew Elise would never do anything malicious to Azai, but their mother would. Lenae seemed to make it a priority of hers to get under Envie's skin whenever she could. Instead of having the bond a mother and daughter should have, Lenae treated Envie as if she were her enemy. Like she was some bitch off the streets that she had beef with. Their relationship was toxic, and Envie vowed that after tonight, she was cutting her off completely. That's if she didn't put hands on her first.

"Look, I'm just stressed out, okay? I'm not blaming you, but you know how me and that woman's relationship is. She doesn't like me, and regardless if Azai is her grandson, she treats him like he isn't. Her dropping him off at Misha's knowing that girl hates me is proof she was on some scandalous shit."

"Ms. Lenae gon' make me whoop her ass too," Zari chimed in, making Envie shake her head.

"Nah. She'll get hers. Moving how she does, I'm sure karma can't wait to catch up with her," Envie said. "Where she at anyway?"

Elise shrugged. "I don't know. She didn't answer the phone the times I called."

"Of course she didn't," Envie grumbled. "It's okay. She can't hide forever."

Envie couldn't promise the next time she saw her mama that she'd handle her as the woman who gave birth to her. As a mother herself, Envie's number one priority was always Azai. For her to put him in harm's way due to her jealousy was unforgivable. Looking over at her son, Envie relaxed in the chair next to his bed. Her night of fun was ruined, and unbeknownst to everyone in the room, she and Zari weren't the only ones whose night took a turn for the worst.

$$\$ \$ \$$$

I n the basement of the old car shop, Misani was seething mad that she had just verbally signed the deal with the devil himself. Scar stared at her with a wicked grin on his face knowing he had her exactly where he wanted her. Regret was written all over her face, but what he didn't see was the revenge stirring in her belly. He was going to pay for shooting Malachi; she'd bet her life on that.

"I look forward to the that phone call," Scar told her and grinned.

"Fuck you," Misani spat. "Bring your ass on."

Shoving Malachi in the head, she forced him to walk ahead of her. With a burning sensation in his shoulder, Malachi groaned as he headed toward the exit. He didn't expect Scar to shoot him, but neither had he expected for his sister to pop up. He knew he had some explaining to do, but so did she.

Misani's eyes skirted across the room as she backpedaled toward the door. Keegan was now on her feet and rubbing at her sore wrists that had been chained. She felt horrible for having Misani once again come to her rescue, but she had no one else. The woman she should've been able to trust had betrayed her long before now and was the reason she was in this predicament in the first place.

"You good?" Ramzi asked her, and she nodded. "A'ight. Let's get you out of here."

Ramzi had never felt any remorse for any of his sins until now. Having had Keegan snatched up, he now knew that the only reason she had been was because of her thieving ass mother.

"Let your mother know when you see her that she still owes me," Scar spoke, speaking of Chrissy. She'd gone missing in action the minute she and her junky of a friend stole from him and killed his worker.

"I'm letting you know now that her mama is off limits," Ramzi said coolly.

"Says who? Was it your shit she stole or mine?"

"I don't give a fuck whose work it was. You touch her and you gon' have to see me."

Scar chuckled. "That must be a nice piece of pussy if you're willing to go against the code."

"Fuck the code. You broke it demanding money for some shit that you could've easily gotten back. I'm not about to go back and forth with you, though. Disrespect her or me again and you won't have to worry about the fucking code, nigga."

The tone of his voice had Keegan tugging on his hand. She knew his threat wasn't a silent one, but he was outnumbered. The gunmen standing around seemed to only take orders from Scar, and she'd never be able to forgive herself if she got him killed. She'd already caused enough issues as is.

Smirking, Scar nodded his head. "Hope you know what you're doing."

"Don't worry about me, mothafucka. Come on," he said making Keegan walk in front of him.

He walked out of the building with not an ounce of fear knowing his back was turned to Scar. Once outside near his car, he turned toward Keegan. The fear in her eyes was now gone and replaced with guilt.

"I'm sorry I keep putting you in situations to save me," she said with a sigh.

"It's all good. Better me than someone else, right?"

The humor in his voice made Keegan give him a soft smile. Looking up at him, she assessed his handsome features under the moonlight. Even in the darkness of the night with a hoodie now tossed over his head, Ramzi was still fine. Dangerously fine, the type Keegan knew she needed to stay her ass away from. But, somehow, the two kept meeting up in unfortunate situations. It had to be fate; she wasn't going to consider it anything else.

"Right," she muttered. "So, um, thank you again. I don't know what you did with—"

"Don't worry about all that. Are you good? Did they hurt you?"

Keegan shook her head. "No, I'm fine. Just a bit shook up that's all."

"That's to be expected. Is she your ride?" Ramzi tilted his head towards Misani's ride.

"Yeah. I should get going. I know she's beyond pissed at me."

"She a real friend for coming through for you. Even if she is mad, she loves you; that's for sure," Ramzi noted. Misani was as solid as they came.

"Yeah. She certainly is. Thank you again," she mumbled lowly, taking all of him in. She wasn't sure when he'd end up rescuing her again, so she wanted to embed him in her mind.

Ramzi gave her a nod before she turned away. His eyes stayed trained on her until she climbed in the front seat of Misani's car. Even with knowing the drama that came along with her, Ramzi couldn't help but become more interested in the damsel in distress. He'd seemed to always be the type of man to save women, employing them at the club if need be. For Keegan, he was ready to lay his cape to rest. Chuckling at how both encounters with her could've turned deadly, Ramzi knew if he saw her again, he wasn't letting her out of his sight.

Inside Misani's ride, Malachi groaned and moaned from the backseat. He'd never been shot before, and the bullet lodged in his shoulder was making him weak.

"Shut up with all that!" Misani yelled, speeding down the highway. "Your ass knows better!"

"Sis, c'mon. I ain't trying to hear that right now."

"You think I give a fuck what you trying to hear! Huh? I'd shoot you myself if I could. What are you in the streets for? I take good care of you. You don't want for a damn thing, Malachi, but you're willing to risk your life for what! For what, huh?!"

Misani was so mad, her vision was blurry. She already had enough on her plate with Carlo, and now Malachi wanted to fake like he was some thug. If she had it her way, she'd let that bullet stay stuck in his damn shoulder until she felt like it needed to be removed.

"I was tired of not having my own money," he mumbled, and Misani sucked her teeth.

"So you call yourself doing what? Being a yes man? Answering to some nigga who clearly doesn't care if you live or die?" She chuckled and switched lanes. "I hope you learned your lesson. I really do. You're moving your ass in with me, and you better hope and pray I let you do anything."

"Man," he groaned. "You tripping. I'm grown."

"Grown and dumb. You heard what I said, so there's no point in trying to argue with me."

Malachi sucked his teeth. "You gon' take me to the hospital?"

"See what I mean? Dumb. Why would I take you to the hospital with a gunshot wound? You want to be questioned by the police? Just sit back and be quiet. I'm so mad right now, hearing you huff and groan is pissing me off even more."

"Man, whatever," he mumbled but didn't say anything else.

Keegan was quiet as a mouse. She had been lectured more than a few times by Misani and knew tonight was one of those nights where she didn't want to feel the heat. When they made it into the city, Misani had to break the silence.

"Where am I taking you?" she asked Keegan.

"Um, I don't know. I'm kind of scared to go back to my house. That's where they snatched me up at."

"Didn't we discuss you moving weeks ago?" Misani glanced her way as they came to a red light. When Keegan slowly nodded, Misani just shook her head.

She was exhausted and preaching to Keegan tonight wasn't going to happen. Had the people in her life just listened to her sometimes, she was sure half the shit they were into wouldn't be happening.

"Can I stay with you? I'll start looking for places in the morning."

"Don't start now. Should've been doing that before they snatched your ass up," Misani spoke calmly.

Keegan sighed. "I'm sorry, okay? I know I'm a burden, but I'll be out your way the minute I'm in my new place."

"You're not a burden, so hush. I love you, and I want the best for you. Had I not, you'd still be back there chained up. You just have to make smarter decisions. Both of y'all," she chuckled. "Hell, all of us."

All that preaching she was doing, and Misani was in the same predicament. The lifestyle she lived wasn't safe by far; tonight proved that. The only man she'd fallen for had looked at her like she didn't mean shit to him. Carlo pulled a gun on her, and she knew had Monae not been there, he would've shot her dead. The look in his eyes told her so.

Blinking back tears of frustration, Misani cruised home with a wounded spirit. She'd never felt so conflicted in her life. The lifestyle she lived provided her the security she'd never had. She and Malachi and those she loved wanted for nothing. All her life, all she'd ever wanted to do was to beat the odds. Her circumstances and her past weren't going to define her. She'd be damned.

Now, though? Misani was willing to give it all up. There wasn't enough money in the world that she'd sacrifice her sanity for. No matter how much she'd struggled to get to where she was or the losses she'd taken along the way, Misani vowed to do it all over again and start from the bottom if she had to.

Pulling up to her home, Misani parked in the garage and exhaled. She thought she'd never make it home, and thanked God she had.

"You gone take this bullet out my shoulder?" Malachi asked, interrupting her thoughts.

"Yeah. Give me a second. You're getting my seats cleaned too."

Malachi climbed from the car making a bunch of noise Misani knew would only grow louder once she started to remove the bullet. For now, he was just going to have to apply pressure. Keegan didn't bother getting out of the car. Not yet at least. Though what had just gone down was enough to blow anyone's night, she'd picked up on Misani's distant vibe.

"You okay?" Keegan asked in a meek voice.

Misani was facing straight ahead, lost in her own thoughts yet again. She couldn't shake the image of disgust Carlo had on his face out of her mind. Nor the tears in Monae's eyes asking for her mother. Unfortunately, she knew the young girl would never see her mother again, and that crushed her soul. The fact that she was even involved with discarding the evidence of her life made Misani's stomach churn. Had this been anyone else, someone not related to Carlo, she'd feel totally different.

"Yeah," she tried replying evenly, but her voice cracked.

Leaning her way, Keegan gave her a hug and didn't let go for a while. She and Misani's hearts were both heavy and knew they were into some deep shit. Instead of discussing it, facing the truth of their actions tonight, they let silence consume them as their thoughts echoed loudly inside their heads.

Tonight, she wasn't okay. Misani hated the way her emotions had gotten the best of her. Hated how fucked up everything seemed to be happening all of sudden. Tomorrow, though? It was a new day. One she planned on using to her advantage and starting fresh. Her first quest was going to consist of getting to the bottom of tonight's clean up. Misani hoped Xander had some answers because she needed them; desperately.

$$\$\$\$$$

"Can I get you anything to drink, sweetie?" Tisha, Xander's wife, asked Misani.

"Yes, please."

"Sure thing," she replied, walking around the spacious kitchen as Misani took a seat at one of the bar stools.

The night before, sleep hadn't come easily. It almost didn't show its face. Misani's eyes closed around seven A.M., and she was opening them by eleven this morning. After patching up Malachi's wound, she soaked in the tub before scrubbing her skin raw inside her walk-in shower. When she was done, she sent Xander a text letting him know her mission was a failed one and that they needed to meet. So, here she was.

Fatigue oozed from her pores as she accepted the piping hot cup of lemon-ginger green tea. Had she known Xander would be on a business call upon her arrival, she would've stayed at home a bit longer. She wasn't complaining though. Tisha was great company and had become somewhat of a mother figure to Misani over the years. Misani's mother gave her rights up to her father before her father, Greg, knew what was happening. The death of her father in 2007 broke Misani even more, so she was thankful for Tisha.

Misani always prided herself on being the strong one. Whatever role she played in people's lives, she brought substance, light, and love to them. She encouraged and pushed for people to be their best selves when at times she lacked on showing up for herself some days. Misani wasn't tired of being strong; that was all she knew. She simply wanted to have a moment of weakness for once and not feel like the doors were closing in on her.

To be able to lay in bed all day with her phone on do not disturb because she knew at any moment of the day someone would need her. They'd need her support, her words of endearment, and a quick cursing out if need be. Misani wanted a change of scenery and not just when she was on vacation, but for the rest of her life. Though she'd leveled up in what most people thought were the most important aspects in life, materialistically, Misani wanted more than just that. She needed it and had known for a while now. What she also knew was that with new levels came new devils, so she needed to be sure she took the necessary steps to ensure she was taking care of herself.

"How've you been?" Tisha asked, resting against the island. Her hazel colored eyes showed nothing but concern.

Misani sighed, exhaustion releasing through her exhale. "Tired," she spoke and chuckled. "That's just recently though."

"Are you taking any vitamins? Don't let my husband work you to death."

"He's not and no. I probably should start."

"Yes, you should. B12 vitamins are what I take daily. It gives me just the boost I need throughout the day.

Other than being tired, what's new? Any new men in your life I need to know about?"

Tisha gave her a gentle smile, and Misani blushed. She wasn't sure if he'd be her man much longer, and probably wasn't after last night, but she couldn't stop the warmth from filling her cheeks and sudden tenderness of her chest. Carlo had brought out a side of her she wasn't trying to let go of. He made her feel, something only money used to be able to do.

"Not as of right now. I'm not sure where this journey with him is going yet, so I don't want to jinx myself."

"Fair enough. Can I at least get a name? Is he handsome?"

"So fine," Misani gushed, and they giggled.

Pulling her phone from her purse, she went to her photos and scrolled until she came to the pictures of him she'd taken while in Jamaica. She hadn't snapped a bunch, but the ones she did capture were all her favorites. Tapping on one where his eyes were cast upward on her from their dinner table, giving her a lustful gaze, Misani showed Tisha.

"Well, okay then," she said in a chipper, yet approving tone. "He's definitely matching your fly that's for sure. Where was this?"

"In Jamaica. He flew me out for my birthday."

Just thinking of the time they shared and how it probably all wouldn't matter now, put a slight damper on her mood. Again.

"That was sweet of him. When you figure out what it is you two are doing, I'd love to meet him."

"I'd like to meet him too," Xander added, walking into the kitchen.

Turning to her right, Misani was surprised to see him dressed down for a change. In jeans and a KC Chiefs shirt, Xander had no plans on changing. Business for the day was being conducted from home, so he opted out of his normal suit and tie attire. Greeting his wife, Xander pecked her cheek and squeezed her waist, before giving Misani a smile.

"Sorry for the hold up; unexpected phone call."

"It's okay. You know Tish doesn't mind me bothering her," Misani said, sliding off the stool to her feet. "Are we meeting in your office or?"

"The den is fine."

"I'll lead the way."

Grabbing her purse, Misani headed out of the kitchen and traveled to the opposite side of the home where the den was located. It was a peaceful setting and not set up like office space, but more so a library and study lounge. On her days of training, she'd spent countless hours in the den sharpening her skills.

Once inside, Misani didn't bother to take a seat. Her

nerves were now rattled knowing she was minutes away from explaining what had gone down last night. In all of her years of cleaning, nothing this sloppily had occurred. Ever. There had been no slipups, mishaps, or a job unfinished. She could only imagine the consequences Xander had set in place for breaking the number one rule; no evidence.

"You nervous about something?" Xander asked, stepping inside the den and closing the door behind him. A double shot of Jack swirled in a glass he held.

"Of course I am," Misani huffed, tossing her purse in one of the chairs. "Last night went all wrong."

"I see. What happened?"

"Whoever did the job left a little girl there, and someone popped up. I was basically forced to leave without finishing the job."

Xander nodded and sipped his liquor. "Did you know the person who popped up?"

Misani wanted to lie. She wanted to so badly, wishing no harm to be brought upon Carlo, but she knew a lie would only get her so far. Plus, that's not how she and Xander operated. They moved off trust; always had.

"Yes," she cleared her throat. "I was dating him and the little girl left behind was his niece."

That surprised Xander. He thought Misani had been some kind of kin to whoever caused her to leave the scene, but never once thought it was someone she saw exclusively. He wasn't mad at all. In fact, hearing her say she was dating brought a smile to his face like a proud father.

"What?" Misani frowned, seeing his grin.

"I wasn't expecting you to say that. Did he hurt you?"

"Physically, no. I just feel so bad about him seeing me there because he didn't know what I did for a living. He believed I had a nine to five," she fussed, getting frustrated all over again.

"It's what you made him believe though."

"Yes, because that part of my life isn't something to just broadcast. You know that. He found out in the most fucked up way. Did you know it was his sister?"

"I didn't," Xander answered honestly. "I don't do background checks on victims, only the clients. And that's to only make sure the money is good. Removal of bodies is handled by Xavier."

Xavier Kyota is Xander's older, ruthless brother. At a young age, he recognized the power he and his family possessed and monetized off it. Bringing along his brother for the ride made it even better. While his crew of men handled bodies, Xander handled the cleanup.

"I know that. Last night was just all off though," she said, shaking her head. "The job was done sloppily, almost causing me to lose my life. Something isn't right."

"I agree. Run the story down to me again."

Misani started from when she first received his text for cleanup, her drive to the home, what she saw inside, how she pulled Monae out of the closet, and lastly, how Carlo popped up ready to end her life with ease. Her breath hitched, and eyes stung retelling the events.

"Where'd you go when you left, because I didn't hear from you until hours later."

"Well," Misani said, now taking a seat. "I ran into a guy named Scar. Do you know him?"

Xander's jaw ticked. "I do."

"Enemies?"

"You could say that. What did he want from you?"

"You. My friend Keegan was snatched up by him and I had to pay him to let her go. Apparently, her mother stole from him and some other bullshit. When I got there, Malachi was there. He's been working for him for a few months and Scar wouldn't let me pay the debt of them both. I wasn't willing to negotiate at first, but he shot Malachi."

"And forced your hand to make a deal."

It wasn't a question. Xander knew all too well how Scar operated, but this was new. Something much deeper was going on, and he was going to get to the bottom of it before the day was over.

"Yes. I'd never betray you, but my loyalty will always be to my brother."

Xander nodded. "As it should be, but where's his? If he works for him, I'm sure Scar had inside access to you through him even if it wasn't direct."

"Yeah, more than likely. That's what's pissing me off. He said he wants to connect with you as if he already knew who you were and what I do."

Scar knew just enough to get the people he needed in a position to send a message to Xander. When their business first started taking off, Scar had become envious of the brothers' success and wanted in. Xavier didn't mind, knowing it'd bring them more money, but Xander wasn't with it. He could tell right away that Scar was a snake. A leech. He only cared about himself and placed himself in situations that were beneficial for him, not a team. It was a wonder how his crew stayed afloat all these years.

"He knows me. The old me. It's an old beef we had, but I guess he's still in his feelings." Xander chuckled.

"Well, I don't want to be a part of it. The people I love are in harm's way now, and taking that mission fucked up something good I had going on. What he's not about to do is play with me about my money or my family. I promise you that."

"I can tell. What do you want me to do?"

Misani tossed her hands in the air. "Something. My cover is blown, my little brother is in the streets, and Carlo is pissed at me for doing my job. I want to know what happened to his sister. Can you get that information for me?"

Xander looked on as Misani wore her emotions all over her face. She was frustrated, angry, and more than anything saddened that she was put in such a fucked up situation. This wouldn't be the first time it happened, but if she had her way it'd be the last.

"I can't make any promises, but I'll see what I can do."

She sighed. "Fine. I also need to take some personal time. I need time to think if this is still what I want to do in life."

"You must really like this Carlo guy," he mused, delighted that she'd found something besides money to keep her interest.

"Yeah, I do, but you see where that got me. How was Tish able to deal with you knowing what you do?"

"I made her happy."

Misani blinked. "That's it?"

"Yep. Regardless of the shit going on in my business and the streets, she was always my number one priority. If my home front wasn't secure there was no way I could move the way I did. This journey called life has its up and downs. People who won't be by your side for the lows but there for the highs. Every day won't be a good day. You gotta tap into something that brings you peace. Something that makes you happy besides the materialistic things in life. Those can be replaced. Someone who sees the good in you and wants the absolute best for you can't be replaced. You gotta learn to prioritize the people, things and situations in your life that are most beneficial, placing them first, to everything else falling in line last. If someone or something makes you happy, then let them. Make that a goal of yours. Your happiness in life determines how you handle everyone and everything else thrown your way. My happiness was dependent on Tisha's, and I learned quickly that if she wasn't being fulfilled in our relationship, everything else around me would crumble."

Misani let his words settle deep in her soul. His underlying message let her know exactly what she needed to do. For so long, her doing for others brought her a joy she'd always wanted. Being a provider and selfless as she could was how she raised herself. The woes of life roughened her up but didn't terrorize her spirit. She gave and gave until there was hardly anything left of herself, like now, but that's how she learned to survive.

Carlo did make her happy. Happier than she could ever remember being thanks to another human being, let alone a man. Not even her friends could compare to what they shared, and she cherished that. She wanted to hold every moment she experienced with him to herself because it was that sacred.

She knew finding out the details of what happened to

Marisa wouldn't change that she was there, but she hoped it brought him some peace. He'd gone out of his way since they met to make her smile, and she wanted to at least put his worries at ease – if only for a little while.

"I hope he's as understanding as Tish is," Misani chuckled, really hoping so.

"If not, you can't fault him. Not everyone is accustomed to the lifestyle we live, nor do they condone it."

"That's true," she sighed. "So, what about Scar?"

"I'll take care of him. In the meantime, I'ma get you some security. You and the girls. Is that alright?"

Misani nodded. "Yes. Don't let them be so obvious though. I like grocery shopping and rummaging through Target's clearance aisles without someone hovering over me."

Xander chuckled. "Got you. Any plans for the day?"

"Yep. Going back home to set some ground rules for Malachi."

"I'm proud of you. Let me know how that goes and remember what I said. You come first. Take some weeks off and enjoy it."

Grabbing her purse up, Misani stood. "I will. Thank you for not tossing me out of the family," she chuckled.

"Never. We're locked in and family for life."

Giving him a genuine smile, Misani let him know she'd talk to him later and headed out the door. After saying her goodbyes to Tisha, she climbed in her car just as the chime on her phone went off. Pulling her phone from her purse, Misani smiled at the extra ten thousand dollars Xander deposited into her bank account. For the stress she was suddenly under, Misani felt she earned every penny of that money and was going to spend it however she saw fit.

CHAPTER TWO

Absent-mindedly, Keegan rotated Ramzi's fancy business card between her manicured fingers, with contemplation plaguing her mind. It'd been a few days since her kidnapping and all she could think about was him. He consumed every thought, which was a bit scary for her. How he seemed to be everywhere at the perfect time must have meant something. It had to and Keegan wanted to figure out why, but she didn't want to come off as needy. Ramzi had already gotten her out of two jams and she thought he'd assume reaching out to him would mean she needed another favor.

"I'll just explain that I want to treat him to lunch," she said aloud to herself. "That's a nice way to say thank you for saving my ass twice."

Besides wanting to thank him, Keegan just wanted to be in his presence. She wanted to get a better feel of the man she couldn't keep her mind off of since the racetrack. Nibbling along her bottom lip, Keegan tossed her nervous jitters to the side and typed in the number on the card. She'd been holding it for so long, she had it memorized.

The more the phone rang, the louder it seemed to get in her ear. Removing it, she placed the call on speaker just as Ramzi picked up.

"I see you saved that number for a rainy day." His smooth voice crooned through the speaker.

Keegan swallowed hard. The sound of his voice made her damn near salivate. "I guess you could say that. Hi."

"What's going on, beautiful? What'd I do to deserve this call?"

Ramzi was a charmer at ease. It didn't take much to woo a woman in his presence, but only the real ones with ambition and something going on for themselves drew him in. While Keegan was the complete opposite, he was attracted to her. Ramzi sensed that she was slightly lost on her journey of discovering her authentic self, and there was nothing wrong with that. He answered her call in hopes to add even more substance to her life, not strip anything away from it except the chaotic state it was in.

Keegan smiled. "Your superman qualities," she joked, making him smirk.

"Is that so?"

"Mhm. I was wondering if you could meet me for lunch. To, um, show my appreciation. I really do thank you for what you did. Both times."

"It's nothing. I'm not busy right now if you want to meet."

She blinked slowly and quickly looked down at her attire. The sleeping shorts and tank top she had on were from the night before.

"Right now?"

"Yeah. It's almost lunchtime and I could eat. That's cool with you?"

Keegan stood from the bed and prepared to shower. "That's cool. Let me get dressed. Any specific place you want to eat?"

"I'm in the Ward Parkway area handling some business, but I'm on your time. You let me know where you trying to grab something from."

"Okay. Summit Grill has good food. You ever been there?"

"A few times. What time should I expect to see you?"

Looking at the time on her phone, she told him an hour. "That too long?"

"Nah. That's perfect. I'll see you in an hour."

"Okay. Drive safely."

"You too."

When the line disconnected, the grin on her face stretched a mile wide. Rushing to the dresser inside the guestroom at Misani's house, Keegan pulled out some undergarments. She hadn't been convinced that Scar wouldn't sic his men on her again, so until she found a place to call home, she was staying with Misani. After wrapping her hair up, she stepped inside the shower and thought about what outfit she was going to wear.

The weather outside wasn't scorching hot yet, but she knew once July rolled around, it'd be a different story. Inside the shower, Keegan let the steaming water flow over her body as she closed her eyes. Her mind drifted to why she was even presented the opportunity to meet up with Ramzi in the first place... her mother.

Chrissy had been missing in action for weeks and it hurt Keegan. No matter how old she became, the betrayal and lack of love from her mother still bothered her. It'd been an ongoing cycle for years and this was the first time Keegan was really experiencing the sins of her mother. She had a price to pay for her wrongdoings, and of course, Chrissy didn't care. The only thing on her mind was her next high.

Shaking the negative thoughts from her mind, Keegan proceeded to wash up. She wasn't going to let her mother's selfish ways ruin her day. She was sure Chrissy would be making her appearance soon like she always did after going on a binge and Keegan couldn't wait. This time around, she wasn't letting her mother walk all over her and if that meant cutting her off for good, then so be it. It was time for Keegan to put herself first.

With her body swathed in a fluffy towel, Keegan removed a yellow and white striped button-down dress that stopped a little above her knees from the closet, along with a pair of white strappy heels that tied around her ankles. She wanted to be comfortable but cute for a lunch date. Giving an approving nod of her outfit, she went back inside the restroom to lotion down, brush her teeth, do her facial routine, and tackle her hair.

Spraying her hair with water, she sculpted a sleek ponytail full of coils in her head after the first try without snapping her holder. Her efforts made her high cheek-bones more prominent, along with those large brown eyes and arched brows. After applying some gloss, she spritzed herself with perfume before heading out the door. As nervous as she was to see Ramzi, she was also ready to lay eyes on his handsome face.

She wasn't sure what would come of this lunch date and would be lying to herself if she said him feeling appreciated after they parted ways would suffice. For her, getting to know him a bit better sounded more benefi-cial...for both of them.

It took her no time to get across town, and once she

was parked, she found herself second-guessing what the hell she was doing there.

"Get your ass out of the car," she scolded, not giving herself a full minute before exiting. With her purse and phone in hand, she stepped onto the curb of the busy street and entered the restaurant.

"Hi! Welcome to Summit Grill. Just you today?" the cheerful hostess asked.

"No. I'm meeting someone, but I'm not sure if he's here yet."

As Keegan let her eyes roam the almost empty place in search of Ramzi, the hostess checked the list and called off names.

"Creed. His last name is Creed," Keegan told her and a waiter approached.

"I'll take you to where he is."

"Thank you," Keegan said, following behind him.

Nervous jitters swarmed her belly the closer they approached the awaiting table. Ramzi's feet were the first thing she saw when he stood to greet her. The stylish Salvatore Ferragamo leather loafers alone made heat course through her body. Slowly, her eyes rolled up the rest of his frame, taking in the wrinkle-free black suit that fit scrumptiously on him. Keegan swallowed hard as a waft of his cologne infiltrated her nostrils.

Moving her eyes from his muscular chest, they

landed on his handsome cocoa powder brown face. Keegan blushed when he gave her a smirk. Yeah, she was checking him out, and he was doing the same to her.

"Hey," she spoke, stepping closer to him into his embrace.

Ramzi gave her a quick hug, not wanting to startle her. "What's going on? You look good," he complimented, pulling her chair out for her to sit.

"Thank you. So do you. That your everyday attire?"

Ramzi smirked, removing his suit jacket. "Not every day. A few days out the week, yes."

Keegan liked that. A lot. She could appreciate a man in a perfectly tailored suit as well as a pair of jeans and a simple tee. The waiter came by and took their drink orders. She'd normally order a mimosa but wanted to stay sober for what she considered their first date. She did order them an appetizer to share though.

"You know I'm not letting you pay for this meal, right." It wasn't a question.

"I thought that's what we agreed on? Me treating you to show my appreciation for being there in my time of need... twice," she chuckled.

"I didn't agree to you paying, love. What type of man would I be letting you come out yo pocket?"

Keegan blushed as he stared at her intently. "One that

has done enough for me and I'm sure expects something in return."

Ramzi smirked. "Is that what you think of me?"

"I don't know you well enough to think otherwise, so you tell me. What did a woman like me do to deserve being saved by you?"

"Wrong place, right time?" he challenged.

"You could say that. We have to stop meeting up that way," she chuckled.

"They say third times a charm, so what else can I save you from?"

Their playful banter came to a halt as Keegan blinked and struggled to swallow the dryness in her mouth. *Myself,* is what she wanted to whisper out but didn't. She didn't want to run him off yet. Keegan knew she had baggage that was even too heavy for her at times. She was still going through the motions with the turmoil her mama had placed her in and hadn't yet come to terms with that situation.

Then, she had finally found a place to move into, but ever since Scar had his men snatch her up, she'd been paranoid since. Misani let her know she could stay as long as she needed until she was comfortable, but Keegan felt that she'd already worn her welcome out. Regardless of how much she needed help, she was sick of receiving handouts. She wanted to accomplish something on her own and be proud of it.

"I'm not sure yet, but I'm sure you'll be given another chance to do so. I mean, it wouldn't be right if there wasn't."

"You're right," he chuckled. "What's been going on in your world since I last laid eyes on you?"

"A bunch of mess I'm sure you don't want to hear about."

"I asked, didn't I?" he questioned.

"Why do you want to get to know me, Ramzi? I'm honestly no one important for you to be checking for."

Ramzi was a bit surprised at her question. He didn't find Keegan as the insecure type by far. Before he could let that thought of her manifest, she interrupted him.

"I'm just curious is all. No need to think too deep into it."

"And I'm curious about you. Why you thinking so deep into this?" he countered.

Keegan's right brow raised in amusement. "This? There's a *this* now?"

The humor in her tone made Ramzi smirk and lick his dark lips. His goatee was so precise, not a hair out of line. Keegan tried her best not to ogle at him when they first met, but she had no choice but to now while sitting across from him. Ramzi was made up of a man every woman had dreams of. The wet kind.

"I'm trying to make it something, shit," he chuckled, making her do the same.

"I see. I like that in you. Besides owning Façade, what else do you do for a living."

"Own a few properties throughout the city."

Keegan gave him a yeah right stare but didn't think he was telling a lie. He just wasn't telling the entire truth, which was fine with her. She knew whatever else he was into had to be illegal. He hadn't come down to that basement she was in out of pure curiosity.

"Ah, a businessman. I like that," she smiled.

"And you? What you into besides betting on races?" He asked as their appetizer was brought out.

Keegan struggled to swallow the lump in her throat. She hadn't been back to a race since her run-in with the man who tried to rob her. Surprisingly, she hadn't killed him and neither did Ramzi. He could've and wanted to, but he didn't need that type of heat on him. Especially not for a woman he had just met. The man in him wouldn't let her be taken to jail for self-defense though. Ramzi was sure no matter how good of a lawyer she may have gotten, a black woman killing a white man wouldn't receive justice.

"Honestly, I'm trying to figure that out," she chuckled

somewhat embarrassed. "I'm in the process of moving, figuring out a dead-end relationship with my drug addict mother and finding myself. I'm just all over the place you could say."

"Ain't nothing wrong with that. Everybody's life isn't perfect. I know mine isn't. If you weren't trying to get it together, then there'd be a problem."

Keegan nodded, appreciating his understanding. She didn't necessarily want to vent to him, but Ramzi seemed to have the type of relaxed personality that made you comfortable sharing with him.

"Exactly. Bouncing back is taking a bit longer than I thought it would, but I'll be good."

"You will. Especially if you plan on inviting me to lunch again," he smirked.

Keegan's head cocked to the side. "Oh, is that right?"

"Yeah," he laughed. "I look out for those who make sure a nigga is fed."

She didn't know what the underlying meaning of his words meant, but Keegan was willing to go with the flow. She was in desperate need of something new in her life and Ramzi provided that. Everything before meeting him was so robotic. The same routine when she woke up in the morning, looking after Chrissy, tending to her gambling urges and just being thankful for seeing another day.

Now that she'd been damn near close to death,

Keegan wasn't taking a second of her life for granted anymore. It was time to live for herself and not her mother. She hated that it'd come to this, but in all honesty, the reality check was right on time. Chrissy was destructive and could've easily ruined the friendship between Keegan and Misani. Thankfully, she hadn't and Misani had such a big heart. She'd come through on more than one occasion for Keegan, and no she wasn't counting, but Keegan was. She planned to pay her girl back and find the best gift for her.

Their conversation flowed smoothly. Ramzi listened intently to everything Keegan had going on and admired her more. As beautiful as she was, he was surprised at the type of shit she was into. When they were done eating, Ramzi footed the bill like he planned to do and they stepped outside. It was still early in the afternoon and the weather for it to be the end of June was nice considering the first day of Summer was last week. Keegan knew it'd only get hotter though.

"What do you have planned for the rest of the day?" she asked him, as they stopped at her car.

"More work until this evening. You?"

"I guess I'll go furniture shopping and spend money I don't need to," she chuckled. Looking up at him, she admired his handsomeness and smiled.

"What you smiling at?" he pressed, stepping all into her space.

Boldly, Keegan wrapped an arm around his waist and quickly pecked his cheek. "You. Thank you for accepting my invite."

"It ain't nothing. Don't let this be the last one. Send me pics of the furniture you decide on."

"Really?" She laughed. "For what?"

"Cause I wanna see the shit, woman. You like being difficult, huh?"

Keegan grinned and shook her head. "No. I was just asking. But, fine. I'll send it to you."

"Now was that hard? Thank you," he grinned.

"Mhm. You're welcome. I'll text you later."

Ramzi nodded and waited until she was in her ride before heading to his ride parked up the street. Keegan didn't pull away from the curb immediately. She basked in what she was feeling and exhaled loudly. Dating had been the furthest thing from her mind for so long – this all felt new to her. She messed around with a couple guys here and there, but nothing serious. With everything going on in her life, Keegan hardly put any effort into her relationships, knowing she'd get bored fast. This time around, she wanted to try something different. Ramzi was something new for her and she wanted to appreciate it while whatever it was they were doing lasted.

Keegan was trying to remain optimistic about her future endeavors, but that quickly ended when a phone call from her cousin came through. At a red light, she contemplated on even answering because she knew it was going to be some bullshit... and she was right.

"What's up, Kee?" her cousin, Myles, said.

"Hey. What's going on?"

"I don't know if you know, but yo mama down in The Dubs wildin' out. Threatening to snitch on Petey nem' and shit if they don't give her some drugs."

Sighing, Keegan rolled her eyes. She wasn't trying to deal with this shit today. On the real, she wasn't trying to deal with Chrissy at all, but at the end of the day, she was still her mother.

"I'll be down there. Where she at now?"

Myles looked through his windshield and saw her walking toward his car. "Walking over here. Hol' up," he told her, rolling his window down.

"No! Don't tell her I'm on my way. She's been ducking and dodging me for weeks. Make sure she doesn't leave from over there."

"How? I ain't about to give her nothing to smoke, man," Myles said, smacking his lips.

"Don't then. Just tell her you got somebody coming through to get her right."

Myles didn't want to and hated seeing his auntie like

this, but he told Keegan okay. When the call disconnected, Keegan told herself once she got to The Dubs, she
wasn't going to go off on her mama. As bad as she wanted
to, Keegan knew she'd played a major role in her drug
addiction. Chrissy had a problem. It wasn't going to go
away in a day or two.

She prayed for patience the entire ride there, and God
answered quickly because when she pulled up Chrissy
had already left. One of her buddies scored some good
heroin from her supplier and brought her along to get
high. Frustrated but somewhat grateful, Keegan leaned
her head against her headrest and stared straight ahead.
She'd been to The Dubs so many times, no one even bothered to come see who she was. They knew her car already.

Just thinking of her mama out here on the streets
saddened her, but it angered her more. Chrissy didn't
want to get help and the only time she took the initiative
to get some, she turned around and robbed her only child.
Before she could let herself get into a stupor, Keegan had
to remind herself that everything would work out when it
was supposed to. Not when she wanted it to. All she
could do was keep Chrissy in her prayers.

W hile the only thing on Zari's mind was revenge, she couldn't help but roll her eyes as she listened to this man on her phone ramble. Her mind was already made up and there was no trying to convince her otherwise. With her elbow propped up on her kitchen counter, Zari silently ran a few numbers through her head. It'd been a week and a half since the altercation with Maverick at the hotel, and he'd finally reached out.

"My client isn't willing to go to court behind this. He wants to pay you out of pocket for any inconvenience this may have caused," Maverick's lawyer, Mr. Shaw, told her.

"He isn't willing to confront me in court but didn't mind putting his fucking hands on me. Seems to me that this is a convenience for him. He should be humiliated like I was," she said and hummed for a beat. "Yeah... I think that's fair."

"Man, bitch!" Maverick shouted from the opposite side of Mr. Shaw's office.

Zari snickered. "And, you see Mr. Shaw. That right there, that aggressive behavior your client displays, is exactly why I won't be taking any hush money."

"Ms. Byrd, I understand your concern. I do, but as his lawyer, I have to pursue every option possible. Are you at least willing to compromise? What if he gave you an apology? Would that suffice?"

"You must do standup in your spare time," Zari laughed. "An apology? Maverick can kiss my fat natural ass if he thinks I'll accept an apology from him. No. That ain't happening. You know what will do, though?"

"No, please let us know," Mr. Shaw urged.

"I'll only accept a payout if I choose the number."

"Man, hell nah. You ain't about to hit my pockets like that," Maverick stressed.

"Well, I guess I'll see you in court then, mothafucka."

"Ms. Byrd, give us a second. Is it alright if I place you on hold for a few minutes?"

"Mhm. That's fine," Zari told him and she muted her phone once on hold.

Standing up straight, Zari ambled over to her fridge and grabbed a bottle of water from inside. She and Flip had gone to the bar the night before and she was running through water trying to quench her thirst.

"If that nigga knows what's best for him, he will pay up," Flip said walking into the kitchen.

With basketball shorts and some ankle socks on, Zari took in his relaxed attire. He'd crashed at her place and hadn't left yet. She let her eyes roam his buff stature and her clit pulsed. Flip was a sexy ass man and Zari loved her some him. She'd never admit that aloud, but she did. What made it worse was that she'd been dragging him along for years and his ass hadn't gone anywhere. Neither had she, but she knew why.

Flip's brown skin was tattoo free, abs intricately carved across his abdomen, locs long and thick, with a pair of lips so dark and juicy, it made Zari lick hers. Though his appearance was a ten across the board, his character is what Zari appreciated more than anything. He was a real one and had been since the day he met her. He could've easily flipped on her about snatching up Maverick's chain, but he didn't. Instead, he laced her with some game and told her to hit that nigga where it was really going to hurt him; his pockets. Filing a police report for assault wasn't shit if nothing more than him getting a slap on the wrist was the consequences.

"It'd be his best bet," Zari agreed.

Sliding a hand around his waist as he tried walking by her, she smiled up at him. "How much should I say?"

"Shit, that nigga make millions. Five or six figures for sure."

Nodding, Zari puckered her lips out. She'd been really affectionate with him since everything had gone down and Flip was loving this side of her. She'd normally be closed off affectionately, but things had changed. Kissing her lips, he slipped her his tongue to suck on as he rubbed and squeezed on her booty. She was prancing around in some itty-bitty shorts like he wouldn't bend her ass over across her counter.

"A'ight," he warned when she grabbed his dick through the shorts.

Giggling, Zari pushed him away. "You know I can't get enough of you."

"Nah. You can't get enough of this dick. You don't fool with a nigga like that."

Zari rolled her eyes. "Don't even start. You know what it is with us."

"And you know what it is with us too. Keep frontin' ma. I know the real you," he smirked, gently smacking her ass before walking out the kitchen. "Handle your business, then come handle this dick."

"Shit," Zari mumbled. "Okay, then. Check me," she chuckled.

"Ms. Byrd?" Mr. Shaw called out.

Taking him off mute, Zari answered. "Yes. I'm here."

"Okay, good. Sorry about the wait."

"No problem. Did your client get his mind right?"

On the opposite end of the phone, Maverick was shaking his head, pissed off that he'd even stepped to Zari in the club. One night had flipped his life upside down. He no longer cared about how fine she was; the bitch was trouble. Had he known that before now, he would've treated her like just another groupie.

"I believe so. We just need to know your price, and we can move forward. Now, I'm not saying we'll agree, but there's always room for negotiation."

"Of course," she smiled, and her pussy quivered as the next words rolled off her tongue. "One-hundred-thousand."

Mr. Shaw choked on a cough. "I'm sorry. What was that?"

"One-hundred-thousand dollars," Zari enunciated slowly. Mockingly.

"Fuck, no!" Maverick shouted.

"Well, we were thinking along the lines of twenty thousand. One hundred thousand is a bit extreme."

Zari yawned. "Not as extreme as I can be. Trust me. You see, your client has an anger issue. I'm not the first woman he's put his hands on, but I'm sure I'll be the last. Let's just say, hypothetically speaking, that I have more evidence of your client not being someone you'd find yourself wanting to represent anymore."

"We can't go off of hypothetical evidence Ms. Byrd," he spoke, cutting his eyes in Maverick's direction.

"And, I'm not willing to accept some measly twenty-thousand dollars. There are videos of him hitting me all over the web. He ruined my character, so it's only fair I receive equal pay for the hardships he's caused me. My career is plummeting and it's all because of him."

Zari was laying it on thick. Yes, she did receive some backlash for some of the videos that had surfaced, but she didn't care. She knew in the end; she'd be the one laughing to the bank. As far as her career, nothing had changed in a week except her canceling some gigs she had lined up. She was still booked, her DM's were still popping, and her emails for more work hadn't let up any.

"I understand, and my client apologizes. You're sure one-hundred-thousand is all you want? Nothing more?"

"Nope. That's it. I can have my lawyer contact you with details before we move forward. I'm sure you know a verbal agreeance won't suffice," she smirked.

"Of course not. I'll discuss numbers with my client and reach out to your lawyer once he's contacted me."

"She. My lawyer is a woman and she will contact you first thing tomorrow morning. You guys have a fabulous day."

With a smile on her face, Zari tapped the red icon and twerked where she was standing. If struggling hadn't taught her anything else, it taught her how to finesse. She'd be a fool not to take advantage of Maverick's pathetic ass. In some people's eyes, she was wrong and may have looked as if she was trying to ruin him, but that wasn't the case. Men felt so fucking entitled and Zari hated it.

If he felt he should walk away without any punishment for what he did to her, Zari was going to make sure he stepped on glass when he did. She'd been dealt a bad hand from the time she was born and a mothafucka was going to have to bury her before she ever let a man get over on her again. The first man who was ever supposed to love her had failed her and everyone thereafter had too. Zeek's absence in her life hurt more than her mother, Nicole's did.

While her mind traveled to her sperm donor, Zari figured she'd kill two birds with one stone today. She hadn't planned to meet up with Zeek, but she was going to uphold her end of the deal. Maverick had been taken into custody, charged with assault, and all she had to do was meet and hear Zeek out. For whatever bullshit he had to say, Zari hoped she didn't go across his head.

"You want me to go with you?" Flip asked.

He was holding her driver's door open for her as she climbed in her ride. After letting him know how the conversation went, Zari emailed her lawyer, showered and got dressed. Flip wanted to fuck right quick, but Zari was on a money mission. On the real, she liked money more than dick. That was just facts. Nicki Minaj couldn't have said it better and Flip could wait until she handled her business.

"No. I should be fine. I'll text you when I leave."

"A'ight. Be careful and don't start spazzing on him. Your ass gon' really be in jail."

She chuckled and shrugged. "And, guess who gon' bail me out?"

"Shiiit. Not me. Better call one of your other niggas."

"You are one of my other niggas. What you thought?"

She smirked and Flip shook his head. "Yeah. You saying that now 'til them niggas send your spoiled, crazy ass right back to me. Another nigga wouldn't know what the fuck to do with you."

Zari creamed her panties. "Mmm. I love when you get all jealous," she said, tugging on his beard.

Gently, she kissed his lips and let out a soft moan. When she pulled away, Flip couldn't do anything but shake his head. Zari was more than a handful, but he loved her crazy ass. When it was time to really lock her down, Flip wasn't taking no breaks. Right now, she had some shit to straighten out, but he'd be right there when she was done. As he always had been.

"I bet you do. Call me when you leave."

She nodded and watched from the rearview mirror as he climbed inside his truck. Backing out after him, Zari put on her game face and headed downtown. Playtime was over; it was time for niggas to pay up or shut up.

Inside of Zeek's stuffy ass office, Zari sat with her legs

crossed and hands held together in her lap. Her eyes slowly scanned the dingy walls that were decorated with plaques and accolades she couldn't give a fuck less about. Her nose was turned up at them all. It was comical how he now tried to portray being this pillar of a man for his community when Zari knew that couldn't be further from the truth. He was a monster in her eyes. Always had been, always would be.

"I'm glad you could stop by," he said, rounding his desk to take a seat. "How have you been?"

Zari gave him a blank stare. "You mean since the last time you even acknowledged that you had a daughter?"

Zeek let out a heavy sigh. He didn't know what to expect when asking Zari to meet with him. All he knew was that it was time to make amends with his daughter. It'd been long enough.

"Can we try to move on from the past and start clean?" he asked.

"For what?" Zari scoffed.

"I'm sure there's a reason you came here to see me."

Of course there was. Zari somewhat wanted to see what he had to say for himself after coincidentally popping up in her life again. She hadn't laid eyes on him since she was fifteen. When her world was flipped upside down. Had he been the father figure in her life that she needed, Zari was sure half of the shit she'd been through probably wouldn't have happened. A part of her wanted answers for his absence, the other part simply wanted to milk him for whatever she could. It was the brokenhearted hustler in her that didn't give a fuck.

"Because you asked me to," she stated clearly. "And because you held up your end of the deal. That's all."

He nodded, taking in her facial features. She looked just like her mom, with subtle features of him throughout. Regardless of the undeniable resemblance, Zari wasn't here for the pleasantries. She wanted to get down to the real reason he'd asked her to meet him.

"Speaking of, how'd you get into all of that mess with an NBA player? Did you really steal from him?"

"Let's not focus on me. Tell me about you. Of all the years I've been living in Kansas City, not once have I ran into you. Don't you find that odd?"

"The city is small, but not that small. Plus, I just moved back not too long ago."

"Hmm," Zari hummed. "Interesting."

Knowing he wasn't getting far with breaking the brick wall Zari had up, Zeek decided to go an alternative route. One he hoped he wouldn't regret in the end.

"I know you have your suspicions, but I truly want to get to know you, make up for my mistakes and lost time."

Though he sounded genuine, Zari wouldn't allow herself to fall victim again. Too many promises over the years had been made to her by men who couldn't care less about keeping them. She was willing to give Zeek a chance though. The minute she felt like shit with him was flaw; she wasn't giving him another chance to be in her life.

"I guess we can make that happen."

Zeek smiled. "Yeah? Okay, alright. So, I guess you want to know where I've been?"

Zari crossed one leg over the other. "That would be nice. We gotta start somewhere."

Nodding, Zeek gave her a smile. Happy that she was willing to let him in her life, he gave her a run-down of where he'd been all this time and the best explanation he could for ditching his only child. Honestly, there was no reason other than his own selfish ways. Zeek was caught up in the fast life of hustling and pimping and didn't need Nicole or Zari slowing him down. Thankfully, he hadn't made any other babies while he lived in Denver.

It'd crossed his mind more than a few times to get in contact with Zari, but he just hadn't. Had he not been called onto the scene as a responding officer that night at the hotel, who's to say when he'd see her.

"You went from pimping women to being a police officer," Zari chuckled. "What a career change."

"Man, I know. Figured I'd give back to the community, put some time in that actually meant something on these streets."

"How nice of you."

Zari's reply was sarcastically spoken and Zeek knew it. She was hoping he wasn't thinking that just because he spilled his life story to her that everything was all kosher. It was definitely going to take time and effort for her to let her guard down completely. Silence surrounded them as Zeek sat lost in his thoughts. This was going to be much more difficult than he thought. Zari was stubborn; that was for sure.

"You have any plans this weekend? I'd love to take you out to dinner or do something. I didn't know you'd be popping up on me at the office. Caught me off guard," he chuckled, just as Zari's phone rang. It was Misani.

"Not right now. What do you normally do on your off days?"

The little girl in Zari was interested in knowing more about her father like simple things. What his favorite food was, his hobbies, favorite cologne, what TV shows he enjoyed the most and more. Her heart ached with the realization that she was finally sitting in front of the man who'd abandoned her. She had so many questions... needed so many answers. Swallowing down her emotions, she smiled when he answered.

"Aw man," he chuckled. "Not much. A little bowling if I can with some buddies of mine. I like to relax and cook a good homecooked meal if time permits. These long days and nights here make me appreciate my sleep and time, too."

Zari nodded in understanding. "I bet. We can plan something though."

"It's whatever you want to do. Our reconnection isn't about me; I want to be here for you. Only if you let me. I know I haven't been, and in time I hope you can forgive me."

Zari's eyes misted up and then she thought, "Wait. Are you sick or something? I hope that's not the reason you're trying to make amends."

"Nah, nah. I'm healthy as can be. If I were?"

"Shit, that's on you."

Zeek's eyes stretched wide at her honesty and he chuckled. She didn't know why he expected her to say something else. Show some type of sympathy if he was. She wasn't quite at the stage where forgiveness was her first option with a person. Zeek had hurt her beyond measure and although the trauma of his actions was years ago, Zari still had scars and wounds she secretly needed to be healed. She needed patience, a stiff drink, and a hard dick to help decompress after their conversation today.

"Sheesh. It's not going to be easy with you, is it?"

"Now, you already know the answer to that," Zari let him know straight up while standing to her feet. "You decided not to be in my life, not the other way around."

Zeek cleared his throat and followed suit, standing to his feet. "You're right. I'm trying to be in it now. Is that okay with you?"

Looking him over, Zari became emotional yet again. For years anger had resided in her for this man, but for her mother more. At least Zeek decided not to be there and stood firm on that. Nicole, on the other hand, had single-handedly betrayed a child of her own for the sake of a man's non-existent love. It hurt, but Zari wanted to have those emotions erased if even for a little while. She'd accept that.

Zari nodded and said, "Yeah. That's fine with me. You only get this one chance though. I'm grown now, and you've been a missing factor in my life for this long, so trust me when I say, another decade without you won't mean shit."

Zeek couldn't do anything but grab his phone from his desk and hand it to her. "You got that, baby girl. Gon' head and put your number in here for me so we can keep in touch."

Adding her contact information, Zari handed him his cell back.

"A'ight. I have you saved, so I'll call or text you so we can set something up."

"Okay," Zari replied as he pulled the door open for her.

She didn't want their departure to be awkward, not knowing if he'd ask her for a hug or what, so she just told him she'd see him later. It was the best she could do to keep her nerves at bay. Zeek had so much more he wanted to say but knew he wasn't moving on his time now. He was playing by Zari's rules and sometimes... she didn't play so fair.

As soon as she was inside her car, Zari inhaled and exhaled loudly. Her heart rate had slowed down some, but her mind was still racing.

"I can't believe that just happened," she mumbled just as a text from Flip came through.

Flip*: You straight?*

Instead of texting him back, she started her car and called him. While she had a lot to consider, her first thought of who to divulge she and Zeek's conversation to was Flip. In a way, she valued his opinion and secretly loved it when he got her ass in check. Zari was a wild one; she knew that, and sometimes she needed a little taming. There wasn't a thing wrong with that, so she appreciated Flip and his honesty. He'd been solid since day one with her and she was hoping nothing between them changed.

"I see they ain't have to lock your ass up," he joked, answering her call.

"Nah," she croaked out then cleared her throat. "It um, it wasn't hostile at all. Can you believe that?"

"A lil' bit considering the nigga trying to make amends. How'd it go?"

"He seemed really genuine about being in my life," she sighed.

"Yeah? How you feel about that? You don't sound excited."

"It's not that I'm not excited; it's just a lot to take in, you know? I don't even know this man, and he wants me to open up to him and shit. I just feel a bit pressured."

On the other end of the phone, Flip wanted to tell her he hoped Zeek had better luck than he did, but he kept the comment to himself. This wasn't about him or their affairs. Flip had been struggling to get Zari to not be so closed off with herself and love for years, so he could only imagine how difficult Zeek's journey was about to be. He had no clue.

"It'll all play out how it's supposed to; don't let it stress you a'ight. You can only give the man a chance and what he decides to do with it is his choice."

"How do you always know the right thing to say?" she chuckled, pulling out of the parking lot.

"It's a gift, baby," he smirked. "Meet me on the Plaza so we can shop. I know that'll put you in a good mood."

Zari smiled and switched lanes. "You know me so well."

That was nothing but the truth, yet Zari was truly

hoping a quick shopping spree could ease some of the worries she felt. She'd never been the one quick to forgive a man, father or not, so she hoped like hell Zeek took this one opportunity she was giving him to make things right. Otherwise, he'd be cut off and forgotten like this meeting never happened; Zari promised that.

CHAPTER THREE

From the moment Malachi was born, Misani had played the role of his big sister and mother all-in-one. Though they shared different mothers, she didn't care. Malachi was her baby and she treated him as such. Had she probably spoiled him a bit too much? Possibly, considering the situation he was now in, but Misani knew life had to teach you a few lessons before you could become a coach. There was no way she was about to stand in his face and preach as if she'd been the scholar citizen. What she was going to do though was lay some ground rules.

While she sipped on her favorite cup of lemon-ginger green tea thanks to Tisha, Misani looked on as Malachi struggled to grab a box of cereal from the pantry. It was the middle of the day and cereal was what he decided to snack on. Shaking her head, she stepped next to him and grabbed the box of Cinnamon Toast Crunch from the shelf.

"Thank you," he grumbled, stepping out after her.

"Mhm. You're welcome."

While he maneuvered around the kitchen, tears gathered in Misani's eyes. A mixture of emotions hit her like a shock wave at the reality of the life they were now living. Years prior, guilt used to consume Misani for leaving Malachi in St. Louis while she struggled to find her footing in life. She'd gone through hell and high water to keep clothes on his back, tuition paid, belly full and show him that she'd never leave his side again. And, this was how he repaid her? By getting in the streets, claiming to owe niggas? Nah, Misani wasn't having that.

When she sniffled, Malachi looked her way. "What's wrong with you?"

"I'd be lying if I said nothing. I just can't seem to wrap my brain around you being in the streets."

Malachi sucked his teeth lowly and shook his head. "Man, here you go with this."

"Yes, here I go. Do you know how I felt seeing you in that basement with a gun in your hand?" she asked, walking over to him. "It felt like a fucking slap in the face, Chi. All I do for you and you go and risk your life for some nigga you don't even know."

"I told you why I did. The nigga helped me out." He stepped around her and sat at the table.

"Yeah, and now you owe him. What could he have done that was so grand that you'd do some sneaky shit like that behind my back? If anything, I could've taught you the game instead of you selling your soul."

Tired of her bickering, Malachi stood from the table and lifted the shirt he had on. Misani's eyes widened before they shot to his face for an answer. Along his rib cage was a discolored scar that stretched about six to seven inches long.

"What the fuck, Chi," she seethed.

"A couple of niggas I thought was my boys tried robbing me one night on my way home. We got to fighting and one of them pulled a knife out, slicing me up. Scar came out of nowhere and shot both of them. I ain't ever seen no shit like that up close. He could've killed me for being a witness, but he got me some help and gave me a job."

"So, you're telling me this random ass man killed two people for you and for no reason? He could've just broken the fight up. Something isn't adding up."

Malachi shrugged. "I didn't care. I ain't tell the nigga to pull the trigger; he did that on his own."

Unbeknownst to them both, Scar had eyes all over the city. Malachi was making a name for himself on his own, and Scar wanted him on his team. The niggas he sent to rob him were some snakes he had in his crew that he needed to get rid of. Them jumping Malachi was all a set-up, and he didn't even know it. Scar had fed him some bullshit story about them having robbed one of his stash houses, and Malachi ran with it. At the time, it sounded legit but now he was having second thoughts.

Misani chuckled in disbelief. "Well, I'm glad he helped you out. I don't even want to know what they were trying to rob you for."

"I apologize a'ight? As much as you do and have done for me, I wanted to cut you some slack. You pissed off cause I'm hustling, but you do the same thing. You ain't clocking into no nine to five every day. I'm only living the life I was inspired by. You a hustler, sis. If there's money to be made and you can get it, you do. I don't know why you thought I wouldn't do the same. Straight up, me going to school was only a distraction, but I did it because I love you and wanted to make you proud. I didn't want you to find out cause I knew it'd hurt your feelings like now. You about to cry and shit when you don't have no reason to."

A tear fell from her eye, and she quickly wiped it away. "Whatever. Yes, I do."

Standing to his feet, Malachi pulled her into a hug as if he were the big brother.

"No, you don't. I probably don't tell you enough, but

I'm proud of you. I appreciate you, sis, for real. I'm good out here, but to ease your worries I'll get a real job. How that sound?"

She pushed him away and he smirked. "That sounds like some bs, but I'll let you make it."

"Nah," he chuckled. "I'm dead ass. You already made a deal with that nigga and I don't know why, so I'm good. You made me move up here, so I gotta find something to occupy my time. Your crib nice as hell, but I'm tired of being cooped up in here."

With the help of some of his folks back in St. Louis, Malachi's apartment was packed up early last week. He and Misani had made the four-hour drive to their neighboring city, handled business and came right back home. He was in the process of looking for his own crib now, but if it were up to Misani, she'd make him live with her. Having him close after all these years brought a piece of nostalgia from their younger days.

"There's plenty to do. How's you and Breah's relationship since you moved?"

Malachi shrugged, not ready to talk about his drama with his girlfriend. She'd been sad then angry as hell at his abrupt departure and for a good reason. Malachi wanted her to uproot and move with him, but that wasn't logical. As much as she loved him, Breah had an entire life and family in St. Louis. It wasn't like Malachi was moving back home for a better opportunity, he was moving back by force due to his involvement in the streets.

No matter how much she tried to get him to understand that relocating wasn't the best for her, Malachi took it as her not supporting and loving him enough to hold him down. Of course, at twenty-two, any choice a woman makes that doesn't match with the man who loves her is misunderstood. He'd thank her in the long run, not realizing how miserable she'd be by tagging along with him making them both miserable and regret their decision.

"Hardly is one, but it's cool. She wanna do her own thing, so I'ma do mine."

His nonchalant reply made Misani sad. She'd witnessed the love the young couple shared over the years and hated she was ultimately the cause of their breakup, but she did what she had to do.

"You guys are still young going through the motions, so I'm sure you'll come around. I like her for you."

Malachi smirked. "I bet you do. What nigga I gotta check for coming up in here while you on my case?"

"Not a soul. Trust me."

"Yeah, ion't believe that. What happened to that one dude you told me about? Carlos or something."

Misani snickered, hoping to mask the sound of her heart doing backflips in her chest. "His name is Carlo."

"What's up with y'all? Seemed like you were feeling him. I need me a niece or nephew since I'ma be here."

"Boy," she laughed, placing her mug in the sink. "I'm not thinking about no kids right now. You are enough to look after."

"You heard what I said!" he joked, hollering at her back as she walked out of the kitchen.

Since her meeting with Xander, Misani had tried reaching out to him and every attempt was a failed one. He hadn't blocked her, which meant her calls were going through; he was simply ignoring them and her texts too. That pissed her off the most. If he wasn't going to reply or answer her calls, Misani would've preferred that he just blocked her. At least that way she'd know he wasn't seeing her name pop up on his screen.

Walking inside her bedroom, Misani sighed with relief. The conversation that needed to be had with Malachi was long overdue, but she was happy they'd hashed things out. He was growing into the man she prayed for him to be, and that's all she could do. Grabbing her phone, Misani checked on Envie and Azai. She still couldn't believe that they all had been into some shit on the same night. She was sure it had to be a full moon or something.

Exiting out of their text thread, her finger hovered over Carlo's name in her messages. Had this been any other nigga, one she hadn't caught feelings for, Misani would've erased his number and went on about her life. Carlo was different though. She connected with him on a level that aligned with her wants and needs in a man. His stubbornness was only reminding her that men could ghost women too.

That hadn't been the case, not completely anyway. Saying fuck it, Misani tapped on a few buttons until the phone was ringing with his name atop the screen. She wasn't too proud to admit when she was wrong and she wanted him to know that. Taking a seat on her bed, she listened to the phone ring for the fifth time before he finally answered. Misani held her breath for a few seconds, as her heart thumped erratically inside her chest.

"Yeah," he answered drier than ever.

"Hey. I see you finally answered."

She tried not to let the irritation in her voice be heard, nor the excitement. It was crazy how she was feeling two totally opposite emotions at once, just from his one-worded reply. The line went silent for a few seconds, and Misani sighed. She knew if there'd be any conversation between them, she'd have to initiate it.

"I owe you an explanation. So, can we meet?"

"You don't owe me anything. Your loyalty is to whomever you work for."

"Look, I understand why you're upset, but—"

"You don't know shit." The coldness of his voice made Misani shiver.

Taking a few deep breaths, Misani counted to three and exhaled. "Okay, I don't. But I want to meet up and talk so that I can. You're not the only one going through something right now."

The softness of her tone had Carlo taking a seat on the edge of his desk. He knew dodging her could only last so long before he caved in. It was fucked up what happened to Marisa, and at the time, an explanation was the furthest thing from his mind. Now that things had settled some with no sign or talk of Marisa's disappearance, he wanted to know what she had to say for herself.

"I'll send you an address to meet me at. Don't be on no funny style shit, Misani. You already got one free pass with me."

"I'm not, and for the record, I didn't ask for the free pass. You gave it to me and for a reason so, yeah. I'll see you once you send the address. Bye."

She had to get off the phone before her mouth got the best of her. Misani hated when people thought they did her any favors for her sake. Carlo could've killed her. He had nothing but room to. Not just that night, but any time after that if he wanted to. He could've reached out like she had, but he hadn't and it was because his feelings were involved as well. Was that her fault? Partially, but she wasn't going to let him hold that shit over her head. In the end, she was doing her job and there was a conflict of interest.

When the address popped up in her messages, she copied it into Google maps and locked her phone. She was already dressed, so all she did was brush her teeth, straighten the ponytail in her head and slip on her shoes. When she got downstairs, she peeked inside Malachi's room and told him she'd be back. She thought about letting Zari know where she was going but decided against it.

Pulling into the parking lot of the address Carlo sent her, Misani checked out her surroundings. The semi-busy shopping area housed an array of different businesses. The place she was going to happened to be a realtors office. Checking her phone to make sure she had the correct suite number, Misani hopped out and locked her doors. Stepping inside the building, a rush of cold air greeted her first before Heavy, Carlo's right-hand man, approached her.

"You can follow me," he told her.

Heavy moved swiftly down the hall until he came to an open door. Inside the office, Carlo stood from behind the desk and Misani could've passed out; he looked so good. The white business shirt rolled at the sleeves and unbuttoned at the top gave him a sex appeal Misani appreciated so fucking much. His gray slacks fit snugly, magnetizing the thickness she knew he had between his legs. Her core quivered with arousal but she kept her game face on.

"Want me to pat her down?" Heavy asked, and Misani looked him upside his head.

"You're a little too late for that."

Carlo hid his smirk and shook his head. "Nah. I got her."

Heavy nodded and told him he was out front if he needed him. Misani rolled her eyes and stepped further into the office. Brushing by her, Carlo pulled the door closed and when Misani heard the door lock, she froze in her steps. Before she could make a move to turn around, Carlo was on her.

With his body pressed against hers, the width and length of his dick caressed her ass cheeks in the barely-there biker shorts she had on. Running his hands up the front of her thighs, Carlo acted as if he was frisking her himself. Stopping at the junction of her thighs, he spread them some and cupped her pussy in the palm of his hand. Misani's breath hitched, unprepared as fuck for what he was doing to her body.

The enticing smell of him, the heat radiating from his pores and warm breath against her neck had her losing her mind. Dragging his hands up her waist, over her breasts while giving them a squeeze, dipping past her shoulders, and to her neck, he stopped and placed both hands at the sides of it. Alarm should've registered in Misani's mind when he squeezed with just the right amount of pressure, but it didn't. Instead, her body engulfed with flames as she was pushed toward his desk.

"Bend over," he commanded with that sexy bedroom voice without trying.

No longer in control of her own limbs it seemed, Misani's frame stretched over the brown oak wood desk with ease. Tugging her shorts down to her ankles, Carlo didn't bother to remove the thong stuck between her ass as he kissed both cheeks; he simply moved it out of his way. The sound of his zipper sliding down was the sweetest melody to Misani's ears. The urgency to feel him deep inside her walls coursed through her frame.

"Move yo' hand," Carlo said, pushing her hand away. When she didn't obey but instead kept searching for his dick, he grabbed her wrist and placed it behind her back.

Ceasing all space between them, Carlo caressed her warm slick folds with the tip of his dick while leaned over into her ear. "You see what you make me do? Fucking hardheaded."

A delicious moan fell from her lips as he torturously slid inside of her. Misani arched her back as best as she could, allowing Carlo all the room he needed. Repositioning his stance, he held onto her wrist and slow stroked her. Misani thought it was all good until he started beating her pussy out the frame.

"Oh, oh. Wait, C-Carlo," she stuttered, bracing herself with her free hand.

Ignoring her, Carlo let her wrist go and tugged her body upward some. With her arch more prominent, he gripped her waist and long stroked her like he was mad. Smacking her ass, he clenched his teeth, annoyed at how amazing her pussy was feeling. All it took was one look at him and she was wet; foreplay wasn't needed.

"Mmm," she moaned. "You gon' make me come."

Her sweet voice and muscles clenching around his length almost made him bust. Throwing her ass back, Misani worked his pole like she knew she needed to. Using both hands, she held herself up on the desk and went to work. When she looked over her shoulder and licked her lips, Carlo shook his head and pulled out of her.

"Man, turn yo ass around."

Happily obliging, Misani pivoted in her stance and wrapped her arms around his neck. Picking her up, Carlo scooted her onto the desk and slid back inside her. With her legs tossed by her ears, Carlo relentlessly hammered her insides. Going deep until her eyes rolled back, he filled her up and stretched her wide. Looking up at him, his pensive dark brown eyes stared into Misani's with intensity and yearning like no other.

Everything he couldn't say right now showed in his eyes. He was mad as fuck at her, but her being in his presence was enough to let her know they could open the lines of communication again. Right now, though? He was about to fuck her good and make up for lost time. Besides their time in Jamaica, they hadn't had sex since. That didn't matter to Carlo cause he'd learned how to please her just as quickly in that few amount of days.

"Fuck," he hissed as she rocked her hips, fucking him back.

"You're so deep," she whined softly. Much too quiet for Carlo. Misani was a screamer, and he wanted to hear that shit.

Pulling out some, he plunged into her wetness, getting just the response he was looking for. Misani shouted his name, scratched at his muscled arms and creamed his pole. The harder he went, the more she came. Laying his body atop hers, he lifted her right leg into the crook of his arm and slowed his strokes up. The friction against her clit had Misani seeing double and her pussy gushing.

"Ugh! Fuck! I missed you," she cried, making his dick harder.

Carlo closed his eyes and placed his lips against her shoulder. Her skin was hot as hell and so soft underneath his. When she gasped in his ear, he poked at her g-spot, never letting up until they both climaxed.

In the nick of time, he pulled out, but damn sure didn't want to. Their labored breathing echoed throughout the office, as their skin glistened with sweat. Lifting up, Carlo wiped his forehead with the back of his hand and licked his lips. Looking down at the carpet where his nut was discarded, he shook his head.

"Is that what you wanted me to come by for?" Misani asked once she was off the desk and had freshened up in the attached bathroom.

Carlo stopped shuffling the papers on his desk and looked her way. "Yeah. You can leave."

Misani's jaw dropped. "Don't fucking play with me, D'Carlo."

"Do it look like I'm joking?" He was shocked she called him by his full name but didn't let it show.

Embarrassed, Misani blinked back angry tears and had the right mind to knock all the shit on his desk to the floor, but she kept her cool. If this was a payback fuck, cool. Misani was leaving his office today thoroughly satisfied and was cutting him off for good. When she shook her head and mean-mugged him, Carlo smirked.

"Man, sit down. I'm playing with you."

She crossed her arms and shifted in her stance. Thick hip all poked out. "I'm not about to play these games with you. You either want me here, or you don't. I came to talk and you just had to distract me."

"I didn't hear you tell me no either. Sit down. We can talk. Let me grab you something to drink."

When he walked by her toward the door, he dropped a kiss on her cheek and tugged her arms down. "Stop looking like that 'fore I have your ass bent over again."

Blushing, Misani bit her bottom lip and playfully rolled her eyes. When he left out, she took a seat and prepared herself for yet another man in her life who was stressing her out. Forget the fact that he'd just fucked her brains out, Carlo now wanted to discuss such a heavy topic and she wasn't sure she was ready. Yes, she had initiated the conversation, but the dick threw her off. All she wanted was her bed now.

"Here," he said handing her a bottle of water.

"Thank you."

Carlo broke the ice first, wanting to get straight to the point... now. He had to get some pussy first. He'd been deprived of her body for far too long, and it calmed him down once he was inside her. Whether he bent her over before they talked or after, he wasn't letting her leave up out of there without coming on his dick; and that she did.

"What happened that night?" he asked, once she placed her bottle on the desk.

"Honestly, I have the same question. I was called to

do a clean-up job, but not expecting to find your niece there. Had she not been there, I wouldn't have known whose house I was at. I don't get told those things. Just an address and estimated damage."

Carlo nodded, trying to keep his cool. "When I asked you about your job, why you didn't let me know upfront what you did? That's what pissed me off the most. That sneaky shit is a sure way to get you cut off."

"I wasn't being sneaky. My job is, or was, confidential. We'd just started dating, Carlo. Would you have wanted me to lie to you or just not tell you? Either way, the outcome is still the same. I'm so sorry about what happened to your sister, but I need you to know I had nothing to do with that. Whatever she was into I have no clue."

Carlo wanted to tell her he didn't either, but he had an idea. Marisa stayed to herself besides the few friends she had. He hated to think that her boyfriend was behind her murder, but that's all Carlo could come up with. He wasn't out in the streets beefing with anyone for them to gun his sister down, so it had to be someone close to her, and Brooklyn was the only culprit. He'd been missing in action as well, so his disappearance made him just as guilty.

Dragging a hand down his head of hair that'd grown out much more since she last saw him, Carlo exhaled. "I believe you. I just needed time to get my head right. Otherwise, you'd hate me."

"I understand but don't ignore me. Next time, just block me. Had I had an address on you, I would've pulled up and gotten you right on together."

A boyish grin covered his face looking her way. "You real gangsta, huh?"

"Nope, but I don't like that ignoring shit. I was just trying to explain what had gone down."

"How'd you even get into some shit like that?"

"It's never about what you know, but more about who you know. I needed some money, a better living situation and the opportunity presented itself to me. Been doing it for years and nothing like this has ever happened. I'm just as shocked as you."

"I can't knock that. Tell me this though; had I not found out on my own, would you have told me?"

Misani stared him in the eyes and without blinking said, "No. Not right away at least. And, that's just me being honest. The lifestyle I live isn't one to be discussed. It's dangerous and I never want to put anyone close to me in harm's way."

"So, you'd sacrifice yourself?"

Misani shrugged. "Yeah. At the end of the day, I knew what I was signing up for. Had you decided to shoot me dead that night, then that's just what it would've been."

Carlo's mind flashed back to that night and the panic-stricken look in Misani's eyes when he aimed his gun at her. She couldn't believe it and it took days for her to come to terms with what all had gone down. Realizing her answer was as real as it could get, Carlo was glad he hadn't pulled the trigger.

Misani was a real one. Regardless of the lifestyle she lived and he'd coincidentally embarked upon, it was hers. She'd made a way for herself and he couldn't knock that. What he did want to know was if she had any information about Marisa. In his heart, Carlo felt that she wasn't dead. He had no answers for his parents or Monae and that's what killed him the most.

"You don't gotta worry about me pulling a gun on you anymore," he told her.

Misani stood from her chair and positioned herself in between his legs. "You sure I can trust you?"

"Trust is earned, so we'll see, won't we?" he smirked and pulled her into him by her waist. "I missed you too," he said, remembering her declaration while he was deep inside her.

"Thank you for hearing me out. I have someone looking into what happened that night because it all seems weird to me."

"You got pull like that?" Carlo's brow raised and it

was settled that Misani was really well connected out here.

"Um, kind of. Not in the sense of making everything move when I say, but I can pull a few strings if need be. I hate that this happened to you and your family. Anything I can do to put your mind at ease, I'll try to do."

Smooching her lips, the one thing Misani had been waiting on him to do, he hugged her around the waist. "I appreciate you, ma. You could've said fuck me and let me figure this out on my own, but you didn't."

"Because I like you. And you make me happy," she said with a roll of her eyes.

Carlo laughed. "All that?"

"Yes, because you really brought feelings out of me I hadn't felt in so long. Hell, ever."

"Ain't nothing wrong with that. So you know, I'm feeling your ass too, but you knew that."

"Mmm. Are you?" she moaned as he caressed her booty.

"Yep. And I don't want you to ever feel like I'm not. We had a small hiccup, but we're back on track."

Misani inhaled the cologne pouring from his pores and kissed along his neck. "Yes, we are. And I got you. Whatever happens, know that."

"Nah. I got you. Let someone protect you for a change."

His words halted her tongue from sliding along his skin. Pulling back some, she looked up at him and her heart expanded. "What?"

"Let a nigga look after you; be sure you the one who's good. I need you to know that whatever happens, it's us against them, a'ight? Never us against each other. A nigga was fucked up for the last few weeks and seeing your calls and texts made it worse."

"You should've answered," she snickered, and he pulled her into him, missing her closeness.

"That's the past now."

"You forgive me for not telling you?"

"I already did when I slid up in you," he chuckled and she shook her head.

"I can't stand you. What happens if the information we get back isn't what you want to hear?"

As she soothingly rubbed his back, Carlo let her question playback in his head. There was honestly only one thing he could do.

"We move on and figure out what's next."

"Just like that?"

"Just like that. We can't dwell on it; gotta keep it pushing."

He hate it had to be that way especially with it involving his sister, but Carlo was a realist. The pain would always linger, but time stopped for no one. He'd learned long ago that the life he was given and the hand he was dealt had been mapped out long before he reached the journey. He couldn't stop because of a bump in the road; otherwise he'd never make it.

Misani knew all too well about figuring it out. Life made her grow up and move on whether she was prepared to or not. At this stage in the game, it was all about remembering why she had to keep pushing. She only let her downfalls hold her back for so long and this situation was just another opportunity to prove just how strong she was at bouncing back... with Carlo now by her side and her his.

$$\$\$\$$$

L aid out in her bed with Azai at the foot of it, Envie let out a much-needed yawn. They'd been lounging around all day watching movies, just chilling. With the ridiculous hours she worked and the craziness going on in their lives, doing absolutely nothing on her day off felt good. Relaxing with her baby put her at ease and calmed her nerves when really, she wanted to yank a mothafuckas head off.

Azai had his arm propped up on the pillow, watching some show on Netflix that had Envie yawning every two seconds. She didn't mind though. The quality time with him was always appreciated. It was interrupted when a call from Zaire came through. Envie rolled her eyes, annoyed that he was even calling.

After the incident with Misha at the hospital, Zaire called himself trying to check her about them fighting, but Envie let his words roll off her shoulder. Had Urban not snatched her up, she was definitely laying hands on the bitch and there was nothing he could do about it from jail.

"That's my daddy?" Azai asked, looking over his shoulder.

"Mhm. You wanna talk to him?"

Azai shook his head and yawned. "No. I'm sleepy."

Envie snickered at his little grown self and accepted Zaire's call. She wasn't the type of mother who forced a relationship between Azai and Zaire. Some days he wanted to talk and others he didn't. She never wanted to make Azai feel guilty when he had no reason to be. Zaire was the one who'd gotten arrested, and no, she wasn't saying he should be punished further for not having communication with his son, but it was his reality. And it would be until he was released.

"What up," Zaire said once the call connected.

"Nothing. Just lounging around. What's up with you? You in a better mood today because I'm not about to argue with you on my off day."

Zaire chuckled, loving just how feisty Envie still was.

But only sometimes though. She'd be sure to check his ass quick.

"Nah. I ain't on that. I wanna apologize about that shit I said to you too."

Envie's eyes bucked as she got comfortable in the bed. "That's new."

"What? Me apologizing. Man," he chuckled. "Here you go. Where Azai?"

"He said he's too sleepy to talk," she chuckled, laying a fleece blanket over him. "I'm just saying. That's mature of you is all. What made you have a change of heart?"

"I don't have nothing but time in here, so I was just thinking had I been in your position what would I have done. You've been holding shit down for Azai while I'm in here with everything he has going on and I know that can be draining. You don't need me adding anymore stress on."

Envie licked her lips and cleared her throat. She appreciated his kind words, but she also knew a man behind bars would say anything. As much as he'd stressed her out since he'd been locked up, she couldn't help but wonder why he suddenly didn't want to. Maybe the situation with Misha did have him rethinking a lot of things, but Envie wasn't going to hold her breath about it. The only apology she was accepting was changed behavior, not words that held no weight.

"You're right. I appreciate that," she told him, not wanting to be a complete asshole and say what she really wanted to.

Changing the subject, she asked him what new books he'd been reading. Back when he first got locked up and Envie thought they'd have a future together, Zaire would write her letters. She was eager to know how jail was and he didn't leave out any details while writing her. Over that first year, he'd expressed his love for reading and would sit on the phone and listen while Envie read Azai his books. It was a special moment in their lives he hated to be missing.

"I'm ready to get up out this mothafucka though, man," he grumbled.

"I know you are. What is your lawyer saying?"

"I ain't heard from him in like two weeks, so I don't know. Hopefully, he has some good news when we do talk. I miss y'all."

Without missing a beat Envie said, "Azai misses you too."

"Damn. His mama don't miss me?"

Climbing from the bed to grab her a snack, Envie laughed. "I keep telling you that ship has sailed."

"Yeah, that's what you saying now. Wait until I come home."

"You ain't getting out no time soon," she joked,

making him laugh. "I'ma have a whole little family by then."

"I see you got jokes today. Envie the comedian, huh? Na, for real though. You fucking with somebody? That's a serious question."

Envie bit into one of the zebra cakes she'd bought for Azai and chewed slowly. Zaire had refrained from asking her that question every week like he used to do. She was grown, he knew that, but he still wasn't trying to hear that his baby mama was fooling with some other man. He couldn't be mad if she was. Between the two guys she used to date, only one had been worth mentioning and she only did that out of respect because he'd been around Azai.

Though she and Urban hadn't made things official and were testing the waters within their relationship right now, Envie wasn't sold on offering that bit of info to Zaire. Not yet at least. Not because she wanted to pacify his feelings, but because she knew he'd have a million and one questions to ask her.

Taking another bite of her snack, Envie answered his question. "I'm not. Are you?" she asked in a joking manner, not really caring.

"How I'ma fuck with a broad while locked up?"

Envie smacked her lips. "Boy, don't try to play me. I know how the game goes. You got you a little pen pal in there keeping you company. You ain't stop being a manwhore because you went to jail. Now you can just be sneakier with it," she laughed already knowing what he was on.

Before she blocked Misha and all her family members and friends on social media, Envie would see her ranting and raving about Zaire. She stayed arguing with other women over a nigga who didn't belong to either of them. His ass belonged to the state.

Zaire laughed. "I ain't admitting to nothing," he told her just as Envie's doorbell rang. "Look like you got company, so I'll call y'all later."

"Okay. Talk to you later."

Envie smiled to herself while walking toward her front door. That'd been the most civil conversation they had in weeks and she was appreciative of that. Zaire was going to be in her life forever and regardless of what went on she wanted to always be able to co-parent with him. Azai at least deserved that much since he'd already missed out on having Zaire in his life physically.

The smile on her face was wiped smooth off when she looked out the peephole. Envie's blood boiled and jaw flexed as she unlocked her door and snatched it open.

"Don't be popping up over here," she hissed.

"Is that any way to greet your mother?" Lenae smirked.

It took everything in Envie not to call her a bitch and go upside her head. Instead of going by her house days following Azai's injury, Envie played it cool. She had been way too angry to confront her mama, but for her to have the audacity to pop up at her crib had Envie hot.

"I'm trying not to disrespect you, so I'ma ask you once to get up off my porch."

"No invite inside? I guess I really did piss you off like Elise said."

Envie's fist balled up. "You did more than piss me off, but I'ma let you make it. I don't fool with you and as far as you being a grandparent to my child goes, you can hang that shit up. You gotta be a special type of psycho to think I'd ever fool with you again."

"I ain't no mothafucking babysitter, first off. Don't be having her drop him off to me if you had an issue with it," Lenae spat, snaking her neck.

"I didn't have her," Envie stopped. She wasn't about to explain herself when Lenae already knew the story. "You can go. I don't have anything to say to you."

Lenae looked her up and down. Envious of the body, life, and support she had without her in her life made Lenae bitter. She was the type of mother that was jealous of her kids and had been for years. They could survive without her and that ate her up. She wanted Envie and Elise to depend on her. Wanted them to know she was the bitch taking care of them and didn't nothing move unless she said so.

After her come up from the bus accident, Envie peeped how egotistical and rude she became. Once Lenae found out she was pregnant with Azai and put her out, Envie vowed to never ask her for anything again. She didn't care if she needed a penny at the store; Envie wasn't asking her for shit. All Lenae would do was hold it over her head.

"How's Azai?" she smiled connivingly.

"Don't worry about him. I'm not gon' tell you again to get off my porch," she grilled her.

Lenae stepped closer. "And if I don't," she taunted, lightly shoving Envie's shoulder.

Envie clasped her hands behind her. "You really testing me right now. I'm trying not to put my hands on you."

"You ain't gon' do nothing. You think you hot shit in this fancy house and driving that expensive car? I made you and this how you treat me! Yo own mama?"

Exhaling loudly, Envie stepped further onto her porch. "If you want me to be honest, you ain't ever really been a mother to me. Who turns their back on their own child when I was the one who put food in the house and kept the lights on for us? I'm not about to throw everything I did in your face, cause you already know. What I did to get where I'm at is work hard and not blame other people for my shortcomings. Now," she said stepping directly into Lenae's face. "I'ma tell you again; please get off my property before shit gets ugly."

Lenae smirked. "I see why Zaire cheated and had a baby on you. Misha treats me way better than you ever have. Let me go visit my daughter and grandbaby."

Envie's heart dropped to her stomach. She'd taken a lot of shit from Lenae over the years but never had she gone as low as she recently had. Had she not been her mother, Envie would've kicked her in her ass as she walked down the steps. She didn't leave her porch until Lenae's car was down the street.

Closing and locking her door, she inhaled and exhaled, calming her nerves. Long ago did she stop shedding tears over her mother's lack of parenting skills. Envie pacified her own feelings, leaning on herself to be the mother she wished she had. Hearing her phone ring, she headed back toward the kitchen where she left it and her other zebra cake. She was ready to decline whoever it was calling but stopped when she saw Urban's name dancing across the screen requesting to FaceTime her.

Attitude aside, or as best as she could hide it, Envie answered his call. Right away he could tell something was bothering her. The crease in her forehead was a dead giveaway.

"Who done made you mad on your day off?" he asked, making her crack a smile. She didn't think he remembered her off days.

"No one important so let me fix my face," she chuckled. "Hi."

"Hi to you. I like your hair like that."

"In this messy ole bun? Whatever," she dismissed him.

"For real. Shit is sexy. What you and the youngin' up to?"

Comfortable with him, Envie bit into her remaining snack and walked out of the kitchen. "We were watching Netflix, but he fell asleep. You still in Denver?"

Urban nodded. He was out there handling some business and had been for the last few days. "Yeah. When I leave here we're headed to California, then home. I want to take you out. When's your next off day?"

Crossing her legs on her smoky grey sectional she said, "Depends on when you'll be home. I'm off Saturday through Monday."

"That's perfect. Should I make this a date that includes our boys, or can I have you to myself?"

Urban shot her a boyish smirk and the seat of Envie's boy shorts dampened. He was so fine and she loved how considerate he was. Not many men took into consideration the role of a single mother. It wasn't an easy job and

Urban knew that, so he wanted to make getting to know Envie better go as smoothly as possible. The way he asked her the question left plenty to her imagination.

Blushing she said, "I definitely think we deserve our own date first. Don't want any interruptions."

"Or cockblockers," he chuckled but meant it.

"Right. My baby does not play about me."

"Shit, I ain't trying to play about you either if we're being honest. I should just fly you out."

Envie smiled. "Tell me how you really feel then."

"I'd rather show you, but you gotta let me know you ready for that."

"I wouldn't be on this phone with you if I weren't Mr. Wright."

Licking his lips, Urban stroked his beard. "Damn, I can't wait to see you in person. With your pretty self."

"Thank you. I see your skin all glowing and beard manicured. Let me find out you got a lil' boo out there in the mountains."

Urban flipped the camera around and panned the room he was in before flipping it back on him. "I wouldn't even disrespect you like that and have you on this phone."

"Better not."

Envie wasn't going to let her mother's harsh words or Zaire's betrayal stop her from obtaining happiness. For so long, she valued money as the only thing in life to ease her worries and now she just wanted peace of mind. She was at a place and age where settling down was thought about often. Even having a companion who made it their mission to make her day every day would suffice.

What she did know was that she wasn't settling. Urban was on his own agenda trying to win her heart and Envie didn't know it, but she'd soon find out.

CHAPTER FOUR

"Whew," Envie let out, flopping onto the carpet and stretching out. "I'm worn out."

Keegan cut her eyes toward her cousin. "You haven't even done anything."

"Yes, I have. Those totes of clothes were heavy as hell. Almost threw my back out."

"But it didn't, so come on. We only have a little bit left and we can take a break," Keegan told her from the closet.

Keegan had moved into her new place earlier in the week and was still moving a few things from a storage unit inside. Being the helpful cousin she was, Envie volunteered her services. With no one really supporting Keegan besides her girls and a few family members, Envie made sure she always came through for her bloodline. Though her mother hadn't outright abandoned her for drugs,

Lenae was still very much so a daily reminder of the type of mother Envie vowed to never be. Not just a mother but person as well.

Since diaper days, she and Keegan had been thick as thieves and it wasn't ever going to change. Doing a quick stretch, Envie stood to her feet. She really hadn't done much, but her muscles were aching something serious. An Epsom salt bath would be the first thing she did when she got home.

"Have you talked to your boo?" Keegan asked as they bypassed Azai in the living room watching TV.

"My what?" Envie chuckled.

"Don't play. I'm talking about Mr. Ball Player, Urban. I know you haven't been curving that man."

Envie shrugged. "Not necessarily. He's busier than I am, so I wouldn't say curving. I'm just going with the flow."

That was the truth. They'd been in contact since he drove her to the hospital. His overall concern for she and Azai was commendable. Urban would text or call her when he wasn't busy just to hear her voice and see what she was up to. Envie appreciated that. Especially from a man who had so much on his plate. She couldn't wait until he came home.

"All you can do. I just knew you'd be waiting around for Zaire's ass," Keegan smirked.

"Yeah right," Envie scoffed. "That nigga is so far removed from my mind, it's not funny."

"Good. He had his chance and blew it."

Bringing some boxes in from the garage, Keegan huffed as she slid them across the wood floor. Her two-bedroom one-and-a-half-bathroom townhome was perfect for her. It wasn't in the hood where she wanted to stay, just to keep an eye on Chrissy, and Keegan was proud of herself for that. This was the first step to putting herself first regardless of how bad she didn't want to.

"You got somebody coming over here?" Envie asked looking out the window.

Keegan shook her head just as her phone vibrated in the pocket of her shorts. Pulling it out, she saw it was Ramzi calling. A genuine grin was plastered on her face and Envie didn't miss it at all.

"Ah, shoot. That must be captain save a hoe," she laughed and Keegan shoved her in the arm.

"You stupid. Hello," she answered, trying to guess who was behind the heavily tinted Range Rover parked in front of her driveway.

"Come outside," Ramzi's voice rumbled through the phone.

"That's you in this Range Rover?"

"Yeah. Or I can come in."

"No, no. I'll be out in a minute."

Ramzi told her okay and Keegan rushed upstairs to freshen up a bit. She'd been working up a sweat all day and didn't want him seeing her a mess. There wasn't much she could do though if she didn't want him waiting too long. Snatching off the damp tank top she had on, she replaced it with a fresh one before wiping under her arms and putting deodorant on. Checking her appearance in the mirror, she opted out of changing her shorts before going back downstairs.

"Be careful with him," Envie told her.

"I'm just stepping outside really quick. We're not going anywhere."

"Yeah, but still," she said eyeing her.

From the minute she told her how they met, Envie had her reservations about him and voiced them, but Keegan was grown. If she wanted to test the waters with the likes of a bad boy, who was Envie to stop her?

"I will," Keegan said opening the door.

The July heat smacked her dead in the face, making her mumble out a curse word. She hated the heat. Summer was not her favorite season at all. When she reached the truck, Ramzi hit the locks and she slid inside. Thankful he had his air on blast, she exhaled and smiled his way.

"Hey."

Ramzi licked his lips as his eyes dropped to her legs.

They had him entranced the first day he met her and nothing had changed. When she shifted some in the leather seats, he made eye contact with her and smirked.

"What's up with you, gorgeous."

Keegan blushed. "Not much. Getting my place together and trying to stay cool. It's hot as hell out there."

"Hell yeah. I ain't want much though. Just wanted to see you and drop off something to you."

Keegan's ears perked up. "Something like what?"

Reaching in the backseat, Ramzi grabbed a bag from Tiffany & Co. and handed it to her. Keegan gave him a quizzical look, wondering why he'd bought her a gift. He answered her silent question before she could utter it.

"A little housewarming gift. Don't look like you don't want it," he chuckled.

"I swear you just catch me off guard all the time. I wasn't expecting a gift but thank you."

The first item she pulled out the bag was a collection of turquoise notebooks.

"You seem to always have a lot on your mind, so I thought you'd want to write some shit out. Get it off your mental," he offered.

Keegan smiled and her heart swelled. That was the sweetest gesture ever and she had never even thought to journal how she was feeling.

"I most certainly will. Thank you."

"You're welcome. Keep going. It's more in there."

Doing as he asked, Keegan pulled out a miniature turquoise backpack made of calfskin leather. She hadn't been a fan of wearing purses up until a few years ago, but thanks to Zari, her collection over the years had grown a bit. This new addition to the bunch was definitely her speed.

"Ooh, I love this. You have good taste I see," she praised.

"Something like that," he chuckled. "Unzip it. There's something inside too."

Keegan side-eyed him, wondering what else he could've gotten her, but she wasn't nearly prepared for what graced her eyes. Staring back at her were five $10,000 bundles neatly stacked. Her stomach churned at the sight before she cast her eyes in his direction.

"W-What is this for?"

"Money to get your crib looking right," he said all nonchalantly as if he hadn't just placed fifty-thousand dollars in her lap. The same amount Misani had put up to get her out of her jam with Scar.

Keegan shook her head no and removed the money from the bag. "Nah. I can't accept this. I don't know what type of shit you on, but I'm good."

Ramzi placed the money back in her lap. "Trust me, the shit I was on to get this back to you was for a reason."

"But Scar said—"

"This ain't about him," he let her know straight up.

Sighing, Keegan wiped her sweaty palm against her shorts. Even with the air on, her body temperature had elevated.

"Look, I know this money was to pay him back for my mama stealing and killing his worker, so there's no way he'd just give it back without wanting something in return."

"You can't ever just go with the flow of shit, huh?" he chuckled, trying to lighten the mood.

Ramzi didn't like how defensive she'd gotten, but he admired her willingness to not be so green to shit and greedy. Any other broad would've snatched them bands up without question. The thing was, Keegan had grown to realize that money was hurting her more than helping.

"I can, but with something like this? Absolutely not. I don't need him trying to snatch me up again. Plus, that's a lot of money to just give back with no explanation."

"You want an explanation? Will that make you feel better about accepting this from me?"

Keegan nodded, knowing it'd put her at ease just a tad bit until she could see her mother's face.

"The nigga didn't have a right making a call like that, so you were compensated for the mishap in judgment."

"What about my mama? I don't want anything happening to her."

Ramzi could tell she was genuinely worried about Chrissy, as she should be, but she couldn't save her every time she needed rescuing. Thankfully, Scar agreed to not search for her or bring any harm to anyone Keegan was affiliated with. Ramzi was going to take Scar for his word, but if he caught any wind of some bullshit, he was reneging on making him pay. Though they ran with some of the same people, Ramzi was his own man. Besides Greyson, there weren't too many niggas he trusted and never would. That's how niggas get caught up, thinking every man who showed love deserved to be put on. That wasn't how he rocked at all.

"Ain't nothing gon' happen to her. You got my word on that. To you or her, a'ight?"

She'd trusted him thus far, so Keegan nodded. "Okay. I'ma take your word for it. I like my gifts, too. Thanks so much."

"No problem. You got plans next weekend?"

"Nope. Why?"

"I want you to fly out to Vegas with me for this car show."

Keegan's eyes lit up. "For real! Hell yeah, I'll go. What're the dates so I can start shopping?"

Ramzi chuckled and ran down the information to her.

He'd been participating in an annual car show slash auction for the past five years. It was major money to be made and he made sure to brush shoulders with those who had deep pockets. When he peeped Keegan at the race that evening and how tuned in she was, he made a mental note to invite her. Since they'd been keeping in contact, he learned she loved betting on races just as much as he did. To him, they were a match made in heaven.

"I'm so hype. You don't even know," she told him, doing a little dance.

"Nah, I can tell. Glad I could make your day."

Keegan tooted her lips out and Ramzi stopped himself from leaning over and kissing her. "Who said all that now?"

"Oh. I didn't? That smile is telling me otherwise, gorgeous."

She smiled harder, not bothering to hide how he had her feeling. "Whatever. I guess you made my day. I'ma have to write about it in my journal tonight."

Ramzi laughed. "Good. Put that thing to use."

"Sure will. Let me get back in here before my cousin thinks you holding me hostage or something," she snickered.

"I don't have to do any of that. Wait until I really get you alone; you aren't ever going to want to leave."

She blinked slow and smiled. "Is that right?"

"It ain't wrong," he said confidently and was damn right.

Keegan couldn't wait to be alone with him. Alone where she had room to ride his face and dick, she knew had to be immaculate. She'd been thinking about it since day one and it didn't help that she hadn't had any in who knows how long. If she had it her way, she was putting it on Ramzi's ass the minute they touched down in Las Vegas. She would've said before then, but she wanted to at least make the man wait some.

Leaning his way, she pecked his cheek and whispered in his ear. "Thank you. I'll call you later."

Before she could retreat back, Ramzi grabbed the back of her neck and kissed her lips. He wasn't rough at all. Real gentleman like but had enough force in the kiss to make Keegan's body melt. When they broke free, her eyes stayed closed for a beat and he smirked while rubbing his thumb along her bottom lip.

"You're welcome."

Peeling her eyes open, she smiled bashfully trying to ignore the tingling in her shorts. *Damn, why'd he have to do that?* Gathering her gifts, Keegan zipped the bag up and climbed out of his truck on shaky legs. All he'd done was kiss her and she was off balance. Her stomach flipped thinking the effect he'd have on her once she got the dick.

With a smile on her face, Keegan stepped inside and

Envie's eyes roamed upward from her phone. They stretched wide at the gifts in her cousin's hands and she smiled.

"Well, okay then. That's how he's coming?" Envie asked.

"I guess so, girl."

"He gets brownie points for that, honey."

Keegan nodded and headed to her bedroom. Ramzi could get some brownie points alright. She'd offer up all her chocolate body to him on a platter had he requested for her to do so. Removing the money from the bag, Keegan thanked God for coming through for her. As much as she appreciated Misani and everything she'd sacrificed to make sure she was taken care of, Keegan hated owing people. She was giving her every single dollar back and felt good to do so.

Sending Misani a quick text, she let her know she had her money. Misani told her to come by the crib tomorrow so they could catch up. Things were now somewhat falling into place for Keegan and she couldn't be any more grateful. Now, if she could remove this nagging feeling about her mother, she'd be good. Until then, she was going to focus on the positives in her life; it was all she could do at the time.

$$$

J igging to the beat, Zari grinned as she rapped along with Meek Mill to *"Going Bad."* She was standing on the plush couch inside of Façade's night club with five-inch Giuseppe heels on, with a wine flute of Patron in one hand. Life was good. Shit, it was great, and Zari had no complaints. Even if she did, they didn't matter right now.

Standing in front of her bobbing his head with his dreads pulled back, Flip peeped the scene. He and a crew of family and friends came out for his younger brother's birthday. Tate was a live wire, total opposite of his big brother. If you didn't know it was his birthday, onlookers would assume he and his niggas were a bunch of drug dealers the way bottles, women, and money littered their section.

"Ain't a neighborhood in KC that I can't go," Tate boasted, tossing an arm over Zari's shoulder.

"For real," she finished the lyric and smiled.

Since Flip introduced the two, they'd been tight. Tate was the brother Zari never had and treated him as such. Zari danced the rest of the song before Flip helped her down from the couch. She was a bad bitch no doubt, but that didn't mean her feet couldn't hurt. She was already planning to have Flip rub them down on the drive home.

"You good?" Flip leaned into her ear and asked.

Zari nodded. "Yeah. My feet were starting to hurt."

She giggled after those words and her man knew she was on the verge of being drunk. She felt no need to babysit her drinks tonight and didn't have to. Surrounded by nothing but real niggas who would without a doubt bust their guns for her, she'd let her guard down and enjoyed herself.

After the scandal with Maverick, Zari was advised to try and keep a low profile but that could only last for so long with her. She wasn't the duck and hide type of bitch. Maverick had caused problems all on his own and Zari was about to reap the benefits, again, from his mishap. Her lawyer let her know things were looking good as far as her receiving the amount she requested he pay out, and if nothing else in the world made Zari happy, money surely did.

Draining the remainder of her drink, she set the glass on the table. When she glanced up, a smirk covered her face when she peeped Greyson across the way. He'd been in her DMs a few times since her appearance at the club and Zari found it cute. She found him cute, but in an 'Aww, I'm out of his league,' kind of way. That didn't deter him from trying to bag her though.

Not knowing what type of nigga Greyson was, Zari hoped he didn't come up to their section trying to speak. Yeah, this was his club, but Flip would get this bitch shut down with a quickness if he felt disrespected. And over Zari? There was no question about it. Everyone's night would end early fooling with him.

When she noticed him walking their way with a smirk on his face, Zari stood up. Letting Flip know she was going to the restroom, she walked out of the opposite end of their section and toward the restrooms. Of course, Greyson followed behind her. Every man's eyes who caught a glimpse of her round ass in passing wished they were taking her home tonight. And every night thereafter.

The off the shoulder, money print bodysuit was melting over her frame something sickening. She stepped through the crowd like she owned the place and she could've had she asked to. Greyson was so entranced with her; he'd trick off every day of the week if need be. With her head held high, clubbers gawked at Zari, noticing her from her own social media fame known as Rayna, and from those wack ass blogs that'd been posting her since the hotel incident.

Did Zari give a fuck? Nope. Not a one. None of them hoes were putting money in her pocket or paying her bills, so she didn't care what they were typing up for clickbait. For as long as she'd been finessing and making a name for herself, Zari promised to never let a mothafucka see her sweat and she most definitely wouldn't now.

When she was inside the restroom, she touched up

her makeup and lip gloss. Other chicks beside her stared, admiring her beauty up close. Instagram photos didn't have shit on the real thing.

"Girl, you are pretty as hell," one chick told her while waiting to use the next available stall.

Zari smiled. "Thanks, love."

"Can I get a picture with you?"

"Sure thing. Be sure to tag me too."

The chick beamed, "Oh, I was gon' do that anyway. I love your personality."

Smiling for the selfie, the chick thanked her and Zari walked out. Before she could take five steps, Yalina was walking her way looking every bit of fine and professional like she had before. The only difference was the apparent scowl on her face. Clearly, someone had pissed her off tonight but Zari was still going to speak.

"What's up Yalina?"

"Nothing. Greyson wants to see you in his office."

Zari smirked. *So, that's why this hoe mad. Figures.* "Lead the way," she said, making Yalina roll her eyes while walking away.

Unbothered by whatever was stuck up Yalina's ass, Zari switched behind her to Greyson's office. It could be accessed from the restroom without having to go back inside the club. At his door, Yalina knocked twice before twisting the nob.

"Man, what I tell you about just walking up in here," he scolded.

"I knocked nigga."

"Say. You better watch who you talking to. Fuck you got an attitude for? You can take your ass home with all that. We got a business to run and if you not trying to do that, I'll get somebody who can and will," he told her straight up.

Amused, Zari stepped inside and waited for Yalina to reply. She never did though. Not verbally at least. Her actions were loud and clear though. She mugged the fuck out of Zari before slamming his office door with an attitude out of this world. For him to have her fetch Zari for his own personal reasons, knowing it had nothing to do with business, pissed her off. Yalina had been after his young ass for months and all he ever did was stick dick to her and handle her like the assistant she was.

What more did she want from him? Greyson had not a clue because she was never going to get it. Not from him at least. He thought he'd let that be known once he stuck his dick up in her, but somewhere down the road the lines of communication had been misconstrued. Greyson wasn't going to clear them up either. Her best bet was to take a hint.

"Trouble in Paradise?" Zari asked.

"Fuck, nah," Greyson chuckled. "You all in my spot and didn't speak. How disrespectful."

"Boy, please," Zari waved him off and took a look around his office. "I'm here with my nigga and that'd be mad disrespectful."

"So you being back here isn't?" he smirked as she swiveled her head his way.

"As far as I see it, we're business partners baby. I haven't crossed not one line. So, you tell me."

Greyson wanted to tell her something alright. Wanted to let her know how soft her ass was while he hit it from the back and pulled on that long braid in her head. He just knew Zari had some pussy that'd make a nigga lose it and he wanted to do just that. His dick hardened when she took a seat at the edge of his desk. Her hips spread out further and the print of her thong covered mound had him damn near drooling.

"Aye," he chuckled shaking his head. "You bad as fuck and probably drive your nigga crazy, huh?"

"You could say that. But, what's up Mister? I ain't come back here for all that."

"Shit, what you come back here for then," he said stepping in front of her.

Running his hands up her thighs, Greyson took two handfuls of her ass and held her there. It was softer than he imagined and his dick rocked up immediately.

"Did I say you could touch me?"

"Nah, but you didn't say I couldn't either."

Zari grabbed his hands, removing them from her behind and Greyson placed his right wrist over his left in front of him. It was clear she didn't want him touching her.

"Well, you can't. Touching me comes with a price and since I can't be bought, you better cherish that free feel homeboy."

Her smart mouth made Greyson laugh. "Yeah, a'ight. I just wanted to see you up close. You still not trying to slide me your number, acting like you too good for a nigga."

"It's not even that. I promise. Normally, I'd lead niggas like you on but I'm trying to spare you and your pockets," she smiled, giving it to him honest.

"Damn. Like that?"

"Mhm. Just like that."

"You cold-blooded, ma."

Zari smirked. "The coldest. Plus, what I look like fucking you just to make your girl mad? Then, I'd have to beat her ass and she loses her job. I don't want her to go out bad like that."

Greyson shook his head. "You swear that's my girl."

"It is; you just don't know it yet."

Standing from the desk, she checked the time on her

iced out watch and yawned. "Well, I've been in here long enough wasting my breath and didn't make not a dime, so you owe me."

"You got me fucked up," Greyson laughed.

"No I don't. Let me and my girls get the biggest section you got over at the strip club for Labor Day. I know them tickets gon' sell out quick and I want the best spot in the house."

Greyson scratched at his beard and thought about it for only a few seconds. Zari's name rang bells, so having her out for Labor Day during the stripper bowl he and Ramzi were putting on would be a good look. She wasn't a celebrity but the city sure treated her like one.

"A'ight. I can do that. You gotta do something for me though."

"Oh no, baby," she laughed. "I don't do favors. Coming back here was enough."

"I don't even know why I bothered," he said tossing his hands up in defeat.

"Neither do I, but it was a nice try. It was good seeing you tonight. Stay out of my DM, too."

"Nah, that's something I'm not gone do," he muttered seriously.

"Thirsty ass," she joked.

"And proud of it."

Thankfully, she remembered how to get back to the

hallway Yalina grabbed her from. As she made her way back to her section, Zari's eyes squinted at the big booty chick whispering in Flip's ear. She didn't put much thought into who she was, figuring the girl was a friend of Tate's. That changed when the girl placed a hand on his abdomen in an affectionate way that had Zari perplexed.

They weren't in a relationship, but she hadn't witnessed a woman openly flirting with Flip either. She knew he probably messed around with other women, but to see it in person had her feeling a type of way. Stepping into the section, Tate eyed her and hoped she didn't start no shit. He was siding with her regardless but wasn't trying to make their section hot.

"I'll see you around Phonso," the girl said just as Zari approached them.

She didn't bother to even acknowledge Zari as she made her way out of their section and back across the room. Hearing her call Flip by his government name made Zari's skin crawl. No one but her called him that, and she rarely did. No one in his family did except his granny and mama when she was pissed off.

"Who was that?" she asked as he puffed on a blunt.

"Nobody."

Dramatically, she cocked her head to the side. "She's somebody calling you by your real name. Don't play with me."

Flip blew smoke from his mouth and licked his lips. "Nah. You don't play with me," he said and leaned down. "You think you fucking with some lame, ma? Disappear again and you gon' regret that shit."

She frowned and he pulled her closer to him. "And fix yo mothafucking face. I'm sure you were just smiling all in some niggas face, so don't come up here frowning and shit now."

Zari's nostrils flared and her neck grew warm. She wanted to talk bad to his ass, as if he'd let her. Flip didn't play that. Zari could act as tough as she wanted, play games with him and all but he knew the real her. She'd been getting a pass from him for the last few years and he was sick of it.

Unlike Zari, Flip wasn't out here juggling a bunch of hoes on a roster just to do so. He conversed with a few women, but none of them held a place in his heart or life like Zari did. It'd been time for them to make it official, and Flip felt it was somewhat his fault for going along with her rules of not wanting to be in a relationship, but it was time to cut all that shit out now.

When she hadn't come back from the restroom in a timely manner, he went searching for her. Yalina was coming back from Greyson's office and he ran into her. Being the messy person she was, Yalina let him know Zari was in the office with her boss and kept it moving. All Flip could do was give her a head nod and return to their section.

With nothing to say, Zari stared him upside the head tempted to knock the blunt from his mouth, but instead she sat her ass down. She stayed there until it was time to go with a pout on her face. While everyone made plans to grab some food, she and Flip hopped in his ride and headed home. Neither was in the mood to be around other people any longer. It was silent for a good ten minutes until Flip said something to her.

"You don't think what you did tonight was out of line?"

"Nah. I don't."

Flip chuckled. "A'ight Zariella. That's just like you not to admit your wrongs."

"What the fuck is that supposed to mean? You're mad cause I was handling business? For as long as you've known me, you know don't nothing stop me from chasing a bag."

"And that's the issue right there. Not all money is meant to be yours. How'd you feel if I pulled what you did tonight? You think I'm green to the shit you be on, but let me remind you, I know you. The club owner ain't trying to do business just because, ma. If that was the case, he would've come and spoke to you in our section the minute he saw you."

Flip knew who Greyson and Ramzi were. He made it his business to look up and study any business owner in the city. Especially if they were black. It wasn't out of competition or anything, but simply recognition. He supported anything black-owned and Façade hadn't been exempt.

Zari didn't have anything to say and that was a first. Feeling the need to really let her know how he was feeling, Flip continued.

"And, that shit with Maverick. That nigga about to come up off some major bread for touching you, but you stole from him. A damn NBA player. Had you gotten caught; you'd be in jail. All I'm saying is you be fucking with these niggas, moving sloppily like you don't have a nigga right here that'd do whatever for you. Guess that ain't your speed no more, huh? Need some more excitement in your life?"

"Whatever Flip. You're making a big deal out of this shit for no reason."

"Maybe I should have a while back. That's my fault. You hot, been a hot girl for years and on the real you need to sit yo ass down. You gon' mess around and lose a nigga, ma. All this back and forth we doing, I ain't with it. It's either gon' be just me and you rocking together and building, or we can hang this shit up."

Her chest caved. "What? You that in your feelings to end what we have?"

"In my feelings or not, you heard what I said. I ain't with that shit you did tonight, and I realize that maybe a nigga loves you, but not enough. Not enough for you to cool out. You ain't ready for commitment and that's cool. But, I am. If it's not with you now, then it'll be with someone else down the road. That's just where I'm at with it."

Zari's eyes blinked rapidly, trying to take in everything he said. She honestly was not prepared for them to have such a serious conversation after the night they had. But, leave it up to Flip to get all serious on her. Deep down, Zari knew he was right though. Flip was in his mid-thirties and ready to throw in his bachelor card. It'd been time for real, and he had been patient enough with Zari thinking she'd get the hint, but she hadn't.

"You ain't got nothing to say?" he asked when he pulled up to her house, placing the car in park.

"Honestly, I don't know what you want me to say. If you expect me to make a decision now, then that's not happening. One, no two, incidents got you all riled up and now you're giving me an ultimatum. How is that even fair?"

"Life ain't fair. You and I both know that shit, but the way you moving I ain't with no more. We've been fucking around for years, Zari. You don't think a nigga wants to wife you and come home to you every day? Instead, I gotta catch you when I can like I'm your side nigga or something," he chuckled. "You really been having me fucked up for years, but I been letting you make it cause I know you ain't all wrapped too tight."

"Fuck you," she mumbled, knowing it was the truth.

"Say I'm lying? You got issues and I do too, but at some point, you gotta realize that I'm not gone keep getting used. That ain't me."

"I don't use you. You know I have nothing but love for you Alphonso," she said sincerely, but unable to tell him she loved him. She never had.

Flip shook his head, hating her choice of words. "And that right there is why you need to make your mind up. You got love for a nigga, but that's it, huh? I'ma let you think that and get your mind right. Until then, I'm good on you, ma."

Her heart dropped to her five-inch heels. "You want me to tell you I love you?"

"I don't want you to do anything you're not comfortable with. You know that. If I gotta ask you to tell me, do you mean it?"

He looked her dead in the eyes, damn near through her soul and Zari felt herself tearing up. She couldn't utter the words and it crushed them both. She'd never told any man she loved them. She couldn't. Not when the first man she was ever supposed to love and love her had failed her. Loving someone and letting them know it felt like too much of a responsibility. One Zari didn't want to be held accountable for.

She knew what it felt like to depend on the love of a man who never showed up. Who made promises but broke them. A man who'd taken her innocence when back then he showed her nothing but "love". In her heart, she knew she couldn't give Flip what he wanted or be the woman he wanted her to be and that crushed her to her core.

But, as always, Zari kept her game face on. She didn't want him to see her at her weakest even when he'd supported her when she was at hers. Not when it came to their situation though.

"I guess that's my answer," he said after she didn't answer him.

"I-It's not like that," she started to explain but Flip had already tuned her out.

"It's all good, Zari. Go in the house so I can get home."

"I thought you were staying the night?"

"Things change," he offered dully.

Zari stared at him for a beat before opening the door and climbing out. She walked slowly, feet still aching, to her door and let herself inside. Flip didn't pull off until he knew she was safely inside. Unmoving, Zari stood in the foyer of her home with defeat washing over her. Though Flip had done most of the talking just then, Zari felt drained. He'd given her a mouthful and she didn't have a clue what to do with it.

"I don't even know what the hell love is," she mumbled to herself, before trudging toward her bedroom.

She loved her girls, but that was a different kind of love. One that had nothing to do with her mental and physical emotions. Just when she thought rekindling her relationship with her dad would be a good idea, it was ruined that quickly. She blamed him for being so disconnected with the men who'd come into her life, and until she could forgive him, Zari would forever feel a disconnect. One she couldn't afford in the long run.

CHAPTER FIVE

Zari's fingers moved swiftly across her screen, typing up one of the longest messages she ever had. She frowned thinking how if she sent the message, Flip wouldn't even reply. That thought pissed her off, so she erased all that sappy shit and huffed in annoyance while locking her phone.

"What's the matter with you? You've had an attitude all day." Misani told her from the driver's seat.

Zari smacked her lips. "Flip. He calls himself still mad at me. I didn't even do shit."

"You think you didn't do shit; he does. You better take that man's feelings into consideration," Misani chuckled.

"I do, but damn. He spazzed on me and to be for real that hurt. I'm just getting somewhat cool with Zeek and here he comes wanting to throw us not being together in my face. I thought what we were doing was fine."

"It was and now it's not. You gon' be sad if he messes around and settles down with another woman and cut your ass off."

Zari's eyes rolled. "Imagine that."

"Okay," Misani laughed. "You think I'm playing."

"No, I don't. I hear you."

"So why you didn't send him that essay you just typed up?" she questioned.

"Because hoe. If he didn't respond, I was making you pull up over there."

Misani laughed. "That's out the way sweetie."

The duo was headed to Nebraska Furniture Mart. Misani was in the mood to redecorate her house and pick a few things up for Keegan's new crib. She'd given her every dime back and Misani was going to splurge a little bit on her for the solid move. Zari tagged along not wanting to be cooped up in the house thinking of Flip.

"Have you heard anything from Xander?" Zari asked.

Misani shook her head. "Not yet. I'm hoping he has some good news. Carlo has been so down; it's sad."

Not letting one mishap ruin the start of something great, Carlo and Misani picked up their relationship where it left off in his office. They'd been on a few dates, had some late-night fuck sessions, and even some heart to heart ones. She tried keeping him in good spirits but both of their minds always ventured to what could have happened to his sister.

Misani was thankful he'd heard her out cause she really liked him. It'd been a long while since she felt anything for a man, and Carlo did it for her. He was the perfect hood gentleman with just enough boss in his pedigree to have her attention solely on him. Any other men couldn't get her to look twice their way.

"I bet you it's some sneaky shit. You should've called Xavier to see what was up."

"I thought about that, but I'll just let Xander handle everything. Nothing like this has ever happened so I'll leave it to them to figure out what went wrong."

Zari agreed. They'd both been shocked by what went down, but knew it'd come to light soon. The two had spoken Xander up because his name popped up on Misani's dashboard. He normally never called her, just sent a simple text. That caused a red flag to immediately go off in Misani's head. They looked at each other, hoping he was calling with some good news.

"Hey," Misani spoke.

"I need you to come see me."

Her brows pinched together. "Right now?"

"Yes. It can't wait."

"Okay. Give me an hour. Zari is with me."

"That's fine. I'll see you both soon."

When the call disconnected, a nagging feeling settled in Misani's chest. His voice was monotone as always, but his delivery seemed urgent. Having been on the opposite side of town, much further from his home than she'd like to be, Misani switched lanes to head in his direction. Her nerves got the best of her on the drive over and she could hardly contain herself once she pulled up to his mansion.

"Will you relax," Zari hissed as they entered his home.

"Shut up," Misani told her making Tisha, Xander's wife snicker at the two.

"Hey girls. He's in his study," she told them while giving out hugs.

"Did you cook already?" Zari asked.

Tisha smiled. She loved the girls like they were kids of her own. "I'm cooking now. You acting like you're starving."

"I am. We've been in the car for over an hour."

"It should be ready by the time you guys are done chatting. Come get you some."

Smiling, Zari rubbed her belly. "I sure will."

When they stepped inside the study, Misani wasn't surprised to see Xavier but that could only mean one thing. A few actually, but she didn't want to jump to conclusions. Xander stood from his desk and gave the girls a hug. Xavier did the same.

"So, what's the news?" Misani asked wanting to get straight to it.

Her eagerness didn't surprise the brothers. She'd been straightforward and about her business since day one and that wasn't going to change. Scrolling to the voice messages on one of his phones, Xavier walked her way.

"I need you to listen to this for me," he said tapping the play button.

"I heard you and your crew been inquiring about some bitch we snatched up. Had y'all been generous enough to put us on, we wouldn't have this issue, now would we? You got until midnight to hit us back or we're giving this bitch up to Scar for good. Or kill her ass like we should've done."

The message stopped and Misani's jaw ticked. Scar was becoming a pain in her ass with each passing day. Had she known; she would've offed him that night in the basement.

"How do you know they're referring to Marisa?" Misani asked needing more evidence.

Figuring she'd ask, Xavier already had the images of Marisa tied up and gagged on display for her to see. The only reason Misani knew it was her was because Carlo showed her pictures for this exact reason. Knowing she was alive brought a joyous feeling over her, but she couldn't help but wonder how long she'd be alive.

"So, the clean-up job I was sent on was for who?"

"Her boyfriend Brooklyn," Xavier answered. "Apparently he had beef with a few niggas and had some money on his head. The voice you just heard is a guy from our crew but was working with Scar. I didn't know this so when I had them collect the body, they snatched her up as well. Been keeping her hostage since."

"And since we won't work with Scar, he's trying to teach us a lesson," Xander explained.

"He's a pussy for that," Zari fussed.

"Exactly. All this time we've been trying to figure out what the hell went wrong and it was his ass all along. I'm guessing his men got impatient and reached out. That's the only reason why we're hearing from them now."

"He said he heard y'all were looking for her. Who else is snitching?" Misani asked.

"You don't worry about that," Xander told her. "You asked me to get some information for you and I came through. So gon' head and let your man know what's up. I'm sure he'll be more than happy to know his sister is alive."

"My man?" She smirked. "You're funny. I never said he was my man."

"In so many words you did," Xander chuckled.

"You love that nigga?" Xavier asked.

Zari busted out laughing. "Y'all are so funny. And if she does?"

"Then I need to meet him. It looks like we're about to handle some business together and I need to know who's in my niece's company."

Misani rolled her eyes playfully. Xavier considered himself Misani and Zari's uncle but he wasn't. Not by blood anyway. He took them under his wing the same Xander did and would always look out for them. He wasn't completely sold on them working in the family business at first, but their drive and loyalty changed his mind. Misani was more present than Zari, but when needed she was there to help out.

"He's a good guy," Misani offered while standing from the seat she was in.

"We'll see. Call him up so we can get things moving. I'll call some of our people before we hit this snitch back with a confirmation."

Misani nodded and headed out of the study to give Carlo a call. On one hand, she knew this had to be done, but on the other she was nervous as hell for the outcome. With the phone pressed to her ear, she paced the shiny wood floor.

Carlo sat in deep thought thinking of his sister. Priding himself on being her protector, he felt like a failure for not having done so. With each passing day with no word of her whereabouts, he grew angrier. It was hard facing his family knowing he had no answers for them.

Simple everyday tasks pissed him off because he knew he could've been out trying to find her.

At the wet bar in his parent's home, he tossed back a double shot of Remy and squeezed his eyes shut. Hearing the vibration of his phone against the countertop, he peeped who was calling before answering it.

"What up, ma," he spoke coolly, raspy voice making Misani's insides quiver.

She hated to be thinking about sex at a time like this, but damn was it hard not to. Carlo had been taking his frustrations out on her pussy for days at a time. Today was the first morning she'd woken up without him having his face or dick buried between her legs.

"Hey. You busy?"

"Nah. Just at my parent's house. You good?"

Misani scratched her head. "Not really. Remember I told you I'd get some information for you about Marisa?"

"Yeah."

"Well, I got some. She's alive and I'm sure the niggas who kidnapped her want some money, but I haven't gotten all the details yet. I wanted to call you first so you could be here to hear the message they left."

Carlo's eyes watered a bit and teeth gritted. "Send me your location."

"Are you okay?" she found herself asking, then chastised herself for how ignorant she may have sounded.

Carlo didn't think so though. Her concern for his wellbeing was a part of the reason he was falling deeper for her. Misani was such a selfless person, he wanted to give her the world for having such a big heart.

"Nah, baby. I'm not but I will be thanks to you. You somewhere safe?"

"Yes. I'm safe. You make it safely to me," she told him.

Carlo let her know he would. When the address where to meet her at popped up in his texts, Carlo let his parents know he'd see them later. Just in case things took a turn for the worst, he didn't want to let them know about Marisa being alive just yet. He hoped it stayed that way otherwise he was painting the city red now that his woman had gotten ahold of the niggas who was causing him trouble.

Not wanting Carlo to come to his home, Xander had them meet up in the basement of a deli shop in the city. Doing as he did for Misani, Xavier played the voicemail and showed him the pictures of Marisa. Carlo's trigger finger itched, ready to body a few niggas behind his blood. He could hardly recognize her they did her so bad.

Knowing that they only had until midnight, Xander reached out to the number the voicemail was from and they arranged to meet up. The only problem was, they asked for Misani. No one else could tag along. Scar had let them know she was connected to them and was truly getting on her last nerve. In her mind, she had nothing to do with this, but she was going to push through for her man.

Before midnight, Xander sent some of his men to discreetly post up where they'd be meeting at midnight. He wasn't about to send Misani into an ambush without backup. If his enemy thought that, Scar was a damn fool. Like she knew they would, the kidnappers asked for ransom money. They'd already been paid by Scar, but their greediness had gotten the best of them. Plus, Brooklyn still owed them so someone had to pay for Marisa's freedom.

"I appreciate you for doing this," Carlo told her rubbing his hand down the side of her neck.

He wasn't going to tell her she didn't have to do this, because they both knew she had to. They weren't taking any chances trying to send anyone else into the spot Marisa was in. It surprised them all when the kidnappers had Misani meet them at a pool hall.

"You told me that already," she smiled, trying to ease her nerves.

Carlo didn't make it any better when he leaned in and pecked her lips. He squeezed her tightly around the waist and inhaled her scent. When this was all said and done, he promised he was taking her on vacation. She had earned a few.

"Just had to let you know again. If shit seems sketchy, I'm right out here a'ight?"

Misani nodded and looked at the time. It was five minutes til twelve, so she prepared herself to drive around the back of the building as instructed. Xander's men were hidden in the cuts waiting for her arrival and departure to go smoothly.

Right at midnight, Misani was ushered into the basement of the poolhall with the requested bag of money in hand. The security the kidnappers called themselves having barely patted her down, too in awe at the money she was carrying and her beauty. Stepping into the room, the kidnapper's eyes went to her. Misani was surprised to see that it was two men she had somewhat trained that had switched sides. For the green dollar, a disloyal mothafucka would change up quick.

"What a pleasant surprise, you do follow instructions," one by the name of Pusha said tauntingly.

"Was I not supposed to? Save the small talk. You know what I came here for."

Pusha smirked. "Still got a smart mouth. Is my money all there?"

Misani tossed the bag at his feet. Showing not one ounce of fear for the disrespectful act. She wanted him to buck and try something.

"Look and see," she spat.

Her eyes roamed around the area a second time in search of a sign of Marisa. She hated that she was placed in the middle of this and was hoping this all wasn't a get rich scheme. Pusha shuffled through the bills, eyeballing it before nodding. It was all there as requested and he smiled.

"Bring her out so we can get the fuck on," he told another guy.

Misani held her breath as they walked Marisa through the door. She could hardly stand up in the baggy clothes she was wearing. There was a scarf wrapped around her head, dark circles under her eyes and a stench to her. Misani couldn't fathom what all she had endured, especially while not having a clue about what may have happened to her daughter. Misani was sure the physical abuse had nothing on the mental.

Pusha roughly grabbed ahold of her arm and smiled deviously at her. "It was fun, right?"

Frightened with trembling lips and limbs, Marisa nodded and mumbled, "Y-Yes."

"Good," he said before shoving her Misani's way.

Had she not moved quickly to break her fall, she would've fallen face first. Marisa was deadweight in Misani's arms as they made their way to the door. She had no doubt in her mind that they'd let her walk out untouched. When they made it to the door, the fake security let them out and Marisa inhaled sharply. She hadn't had the luxury of inhaling the night air in so long, it brought tears to her eyes.

"Sshhh. You're safe now," Misani soothed, placing her in the passenger seat of the car she'd driven.

As instructed, she drove down the street and pulled into the empty shopping center lot where Carlo and Xander's crew were. They had eyes on the poolhall and would for the next hour or so. Hopping out of the truck he was in, Carlo rushed to the passenger side and damn near broke down seeing his sister like that. Cradling her in his arms, Marisa cried like a baby while apologizing. Carlo couldn't speak. He wanted to murder Brooklyn all over again for having his sister mixed up in his bullshit.

Misani blinked back tears at their reunion but got back focused on the task at hand. Looking Carlo in the eyes, she held up a device with a button on it and he smiled. Had they patted her down and really checked the bag of money, they would've known that the money was counterfeit and there was an explosive lining the bag's interior.

"Do it now?" she asked, and he shook his head no.

"Not yet."

Scooping Marisa up, Carlo headed to the truck and placed her in the backseat. Misani cut the car she was driving off and hopped in the passenger seat. One of

Xander's most trusted guards was driving. When they pulled off, opposite direction of the poolhall, Carlo tapped Misani on the arm giving her the go ahead to set the explosive off. Eagerly with a smug look on her face, she pressed the button and felt the ground shake a bit beneath them.

Being a rat and money-hungry had gotten the men killed and in Misani's eyes, there was no other way for them to go out. Jail for men like them was too easy. Everyone had a price to pay for their deceitfulness one day, and death was theirs. Karma had come back around and made her appearance like only she could. Scar would meet his fate soon as well.

CHAPTER SIX

As promised, Urban returned home and was anxious as ever to see Envie. He had fatherly duties to tend to first, but she was on his list right after. So much so that he drove them to their destination for the night with his security following behind them. The upscale prime seafood restaurant in Overland Park had a room with no windows reserved for the couple. Privacy was definitely going to be needed during their date.

"This is nice. Have you been here before?" Envie asked him as a waitress poured wine into her glass.

Urban knew she had said something but wasn't quite sure what. He couldn't make out the words leaving her lips because his vision was consumed with taking her in. Inside the truck he couldn't admire her much under the streetlights as they cruised, but now he wasn't holding back.

The silk rose gold mini dress with thin straps against her caramel skin complexion was breathtaking. The front dipped low and had her breasts looking delectable, while her entire back was out. Knowing a half-bra would ruin the outfit, Envie opted out of wearing one. Her nipples poking through the material was risqué, but Urban loved that shit. He'd pull her closer to him in his lap and suck on them both if she was down. She'd gotten dressed with him in mind and had done a damn good job.

Soft feather curls framed her slim face, nude gloss coated her lips and small diamonds shined around her neck and wrist. The tennis bracelet was a gift to herself on her last birthday. To finish off her outfit, a pair of nude heels were on her feet.

"You okay?" Envie asked with a concerned look on her face.

Urban grinned. "My fault. I was just staring hard as hell."

That made Envie blush. She seemed to be doing that a lot in his presence, but she wasn't complaining. "It's okay. I asked, have you ever been here before?"

"Yeah. More than a few times. The food is fire."

"I bet. Everything on this menu sounds so good."

"You allergic to anything? I guess I should've asked

that before I had you around all this seafood," he said chastising himself for not being on his game.

"I'm not thank goodness. That'd ruin our date," she chuckled.

"Nah. I'd just find us another spot. You not getting away from me that easily."

The intensity of his gaze made Envie's mouth water. Urban was beautiful if a man could be considered as such. As she gathered during their first encounter, everything about him was wide. Nose, lips, shoulders, the expanding of his hand when he reached for her dainty one.

Bringing the back of her hand to his mouth, he kissed it softly, setting her skin ablaze. "Who's watching Azai for you?" he asked.

"My friend Zari. She swears she's not having kids anytime soon, so she treats Azai like her own."

Urban grinned. "Let her spoil him. My sister does the same with Caleb and I let her. He's a good kid though, so I don't mind."

"Same. So, let me ask you something."

"Aw hell," he chuckled. "Why you say it like that? You found some dirt on me or something?"

Envie laughed. "Not at all. Is there some I should be worried about?" Urban shook his head no.

"None I can think of. My slate is pretty much clean, love."

"Well good. Then this question won't do any harm."

"Shoot," he told her, giving her the go ahead to ask her question.

"When was your last serious relationship?"

"How serious we talking?"

Envie twisted her lips from side to side and hummed. "Ready to walk down the aisle tie the knot serious."

He could answer that with ease. There wasn't much time for him to date, not seriously anyway, and he hadn't since his son's mother. That was over five years ago when Caleb was two. There'd been nothing intimate between him and Candice since. He did his part and she did hers.

"With Caleb's mom. That was five years ago though."

Envie stared at him with astonishment. "Really?"

"Yeah. We had been together for years before he was born and she was with me when I entered the draft and all."

"So she was really with you shooting in the gym, huh?"

"Hell yeah. I tried to tie that down and had for a little while. Caleb was born and I guess the idea of being married to an NBA player wasn't something she wanted anymore."

Envie noticed his facial expression didn't change. That was good. She hoped he wasn't still caught up on his ex, because she surely wasn't. Their food was brought out and Urban said grace before they dug in and continued their conversation.

"That lifestyle can be a lot I'm assuming."

"Yeah," he nodded, chewing on a piece of lobster. "It is, but it's more rewarding when you have someone to share it with. Shit be lonely for real. I ain't into fucking a bunch of groupies just because I can. I did that in my younger days."

Envie could only imagine that. She was positive their upbringing was nothing alike. Though he and Azai shared the same heart condition, Envie wondered did he struggle. What type of mother he had? Did he have family who he could reach out to if in need or was his like hers? Envie could count on one hand the people who'd come through for her regardless. Two of them being Zari and Misani.

"What about you? When was your last serious relationship?"

"About two years ago. I consider it serious enough if I bring the man around Azai."

Urban nodded, understanding completely. Having another man around your child as a woman was much different than having a woman around them. Sometimes. It all depended on the parent. Thankfully, Candice wasn't the crazy type and allowed Urban to parent the best way he knew how. She trusted him to not have random hoes around their son, and he the same.

"I guess I'll know we're serious when I meet him then, huh?"

She smiled. "I guess so. I finally told him that I know you and he just keeps asking about you."

"Word?" he chuckled.

"Yes. He asked me tonight was it you I was going on a date with."

"What you tell him?"

"What you think I told him?" she shot back with a smirk.

Urban licked the butter from his lips and chills covered Envie's arms and legs. "Hopefully, you told my man the truth. I don't need him thinking you're out dating some other guys."

"Oh, please," she playfully rolled her eyes. "I told him it was you though and he had a million and one questions before I dropped him off."

"As he should. I can't wait to meet him."

When dinner was over, Urban wasn't ready to let Envie out of his presence just yet. Instead, they met up with a few of his teammates at a club down on Power&Light. Dancing the night away, unbothered by the reality of her issues at home, Envie enjoyed herself just a little too much. She wanted to be on her best behavior while in front of his teammates and the public, but once that liquor got up in her, it was a different story. She wasn't drunk and still very much coherent, but she was indeed tipsy. Horny as fuck too.

"Bae, you ready to go home?" Urban whispered in her ear as she grinded against him.

His hand was placed securely around her waist as her head leaned against his chest. She felt protected in his arms and didn't want to be anywhere else.

"You coming with me?" she asked turning around to face him.

Envie fell into his chest, wrapping her arms around his neck. "We're only leaving if you come home with me."

"A'ight."

"A'ight what?" she frowned.

Urban chuckled and ran his large hand down her back. Kissing along her neck, he said, "I'll go home with you."

That was all Envie needed to hear. Her body was on fire and all she wanted to do was lift her dress up and hump Urban's handsome face. Security walked them through the back exit and his driver was waiting for them. Helping Envie in first, Urban slid in beside her and they pulled off. Urban gave him instructions to head toward his place instead of hers. It wasn't that he didn't trust her, because he did, but he still had to move smart as a celebrity.

"Mmm," Envie moaned rubbing her hand along his

thigh. Her nose was planted in the crook of his neck, inhaling all of him. "You still smell so good. Damn."

Picking her up, Urban made her straddle his lap. "What you touching all on me for," he joked.

"I can rub on you. Your dick doesn't seem to have an issue."

As she slowly grinded in his lap, bringing his member to life even more, Urban drank her in. She was buzzing and the lust in her eyes had him ready to risk it all. Her caramel skin glowed as the city lights danced across it. Her frame fit so perfectly atop his, he couldn't help but bring her closer to him.

"You have fun tonight?" he asked her.

Envie nodded. "Mhm. Thank you."

"You're welcome. We're going to my place, okay? I know you wanted to go to yours but—"

Envie hushed him with a kiss. She'd been dying and deprived of doing so all night. The most she'd done was kiss along his jawline and neck. Shocked by her bold act of intimacy, Urban gave her exactly what she wanted. Slipping his tongue into her mouth, his hands slid under her dress, cupping her bare cheeks. His large hands covered them both and Envie moaned when he squeezed one.

"You got me ready to fuck you in this backseat," he said in a grumble against her ear.

"Fuck me then."

His dick begged to be set free, but Urban knew he couldn't bless her with backseat dick. He wanted her in the comfort of his bed while he stretched her little ass out. What he could do though, was eat her pussy. Envie was so short compared to him, Urban had no problems lifting her up by her ass and laying her against the seat. Pressing a button, the partition he had installed lifted for privacy. The drive to his place was a good thirty to forty minutes out and he had all plans to use every minute wisely.

Stretched out on the seat, Envie's eyes were low and legs spread wide. Urban's hands trailed up her thighs, removed her thong, and stuck it in the pocket of his pants. Not wanting to use his hands since they'd been in the club for the last couple of hours, Urban kissed up her thighs and used his plump lips to caress her slick folds. Helping him out, Envie spread her own lower lips and he dove headfirst into her moist center.

"Ugh," she gasped as his tongue teased her opening before focusing on her clit.

Grabbing the back of her thighs, Urban made her spread her legs more. One of Envie's feet were touching the window, while the other stretched across the headrest. Spread eagle, she rotated her hips, making him eat her pussy as if his life depended on it. Suckling her clit into his mouth, Urban sucked hard causing her back to arch away from the seat.

"Fuck! Yes, yes, yes. Right there," she cried, palming the back of his head.

Her legs twitched and eyes rolled back, but Urban never let up. Venturing lower, he probed at her asshole, showing it some love too. Dragging his fat tongue up and down in a slow manner, he wanted to make sure the smell and taste of Envie were embedded. She damn sure tasted as good as she looked and Urban couldn't get enough.

Reaching under her dress, he squeezed her right breast and pinched the nipple of the left one. Envie was so hyper-sensitive, she came undone. Holding onto his wrist, her legs vibrated around his head. Urban kept on licking, sucking and bringing her to the best orgasm she'd had ever. Period. No man had ever been able to put it down like he just did.

"This pussy taste so good, ma. You know that?"

Holding one hand against the top of her mound, Urban located her clitoris again. Flicking his tongue from the side, he moved it quickly, bringing Envie to another orgasm in less than thirty seconds.

"Ooooh!" she moaned softly; eyes shut tight.

Her core quaked and toes popped as she climaxed. When her eyes finally did open, Urban was kissing her lips and smacking her ass. Hungrily, she tongued him down and massaged his length through his pants. She wanted to hop on his dick so bad she could cry.

"We're almost home," he told her, helping her sit up.

Tugging her dress down, Envie got her breathing under control and gave him a lazy smile. "You weren't playing, huh?"

He licked his lips again, unable to satisfy his newfound craving for her. "Nah. Not at all."

Envie scooted his way and rested her head on his shoulder. "I see."

Once they made it to his place, Envie wished she'd been given a tour of the place, but they didn't make it that far. As soon as they entered the door and the alarm was set, Urban had her up in the air, leg's wrapped around his shoulders and her back against the wall. That night, he fucked her slow, delivering every inch of dick to her. And, she took it too. She was tiny but could take the pipe like a well-seasoned porn star. She rode him reverse cowgirl, bringing him to his peak and they both passed out right after.

Envie had no clue what time it was when she woke up, but Urban's arms were wrapped around her waist as they spooned. She smiled to herself and snuggled closer to him. It'd been so long since she'd been laid up after a much-needed sex session. Let alone be taken to dinner and shake her ass at the club. Last night was everything she didn't know she needed and to show Urban her appreciation, she wanted to thank him with some morning head.

Gently, she removed his arm from around her and shuffled under the cover. His hairy legs were stretched wide and dick lying against it. She inhaled the scent of herself on him and her mouth watered. Before she could lick the tip, a cell phone rang loudly making her jump. Caught off guard by its shrill tone, Envie wondered if it were her phone. Last night after she'd fallen asleep, Urban brought her things upstairs and placed them on his dresser.

Knowing her nerves wouldn't settle and the ringing wouldn't stop, she pushed the cover back. Eyes scanning the room, she searched for her purse and climbed from the bed just as the phone started ringing again. Quickly, she snatched it from inside her purse and frowned. The unknown number calling back to back had interrupted her dicksucking time and they were about to hear her mouth.

"Hello," she answered in a hiss with much attitude.

"Damn. You busy? I been trying to call you all morning."

Envie removed the phone from her ear and scanned the number. It wasn't saved, but she knew the person's voice that was for sure.

"Zaire?" she whispered.

"Yeah, man. Who else? And why you whispering and shit? I'm out and parked outside your crib but you ain't here. What's up?"

"You're out? Since when?"

"Since this morning, Envie. Quit playing with me and bring your ass home so I can see you and my son."

Groaning, Envie palmed her forehead. "I'll call you when I'm on my way."

"You do that," Zaire told her and hung up.

Looking at the time on her phone, she was surprised to see it was almost noon. With the night she had, Envie wasn't prepared for the bullshit she was sure Zaire was about to bring to the table. That phone call and his tone of voice alone said it all.

Shaking her head, Envie stretched and thought, "Why didn't he tell me he was getting out this soon?"

That was just one of many questions she had and she was sure he had some of his own as well.

$$$

"She said I could braid her hair first!" Kenya, Keegan's little cousin, sassed to her other cousin.

"You can't even braid ugly!" Mina, the youngest yelled.

"Hey. None of that. You don't call her ugly, so say sorry," Keegan told her.

Mina pouted. "Sorry."

"And I ain't ugly, little cry baby!" Kenya spat back.

Keegan held in her laugh and shook her head while walking onto the porch. "Neither of you are touching my hair until y'all can talk nicely to each other."

Her little cousins were fascinated with her hair and always wanted to play in it. She was only going to let them because she needed to wash it anyway.

"Awww man," they said in unison watching Keegan walk inside the house.

She just pulled up over her granny's house and the block was live for a weekday. She needed to be surrounded by some love and was tired of sulking around the house. Knowing her granny could put a smile on her face, she got dressed for the day and headed over there.

Walking into the kitchen, her granny smiled at her and told her to sit down. "You know I've been praying for you. He shol' be listening."

Keegan kissed her cheek and sat down in one of the chairs. The dining room set had been in the family for years and she wasn't giving it up until it was on its last leg. Hell, probably not even then.

"Hey, Granny."

"Hey to you. What you doing on this side of town? We hardly see you now."

"Just came to visit. How have you been?"

"I'm alright. Besides looking after those children out there, I can't complain."

Keegan sighed. "That's good. I've been meaning to get by here but been busy."

"Mhm," Louise waved her off. "Busy worrying about your mama still, huh?"

"Am I not supposed to?"

Louise placed a hand on her hip. "Now, you don't go getting smart with me, hell. I know that's your mama; that's my damn daughter."

Keegan chuckled. "Sorry."

"All I'm saying is you can't worry yourself sick over other people's decisions in life, baby. Your mama is going to do what she wants to do and there ain't a thing you can do about it. The only thing you can do is pray for her."

Keegan wanted to tell her granny she was tired of doing that but didn't. All she wanted for Chrissy to do was get clean. Keegan had been praying since she was a young girl. Her granny used to take her to church faithfully. She knew the power of seeking God and asking for whatever her heart desired, but maybe it was time for a change.

She wanted to thank Him for keeping Chrissy safe.

Thank Him for always providing her the opportunity to see another day. Thank Him for not just being a giving God, but one who doesn't run out. Keegan's cup of favors overflowed and God had not one issue. He heard her cries at night. She was His child and would always make sure she was covered, but she had to have faith.

The fear of losing her mother couldn't coincide with what He was doing. Faith and fear cannot dwell in the same place, and until Keegan understood that, she'd never be at peace with herself or her mother.

"I will. It just hurts," she said wiping a tear from her eye.

"You gotta let that hurt go so you can heal and move on with your life. Your mother is holding you back from so much, baby. That's no way to live at all. I thought you wanted to go to school. What happened to that?"

Keegan shrugged. Honestly, she'd gotten sidetracked way before now and hadn't thought about school in a while. "I still want to."

"Well, do it then. The next time I talk to you, you better have some get up and go about yourself. How're my girls doing?" she asked referring to Misani, Envie and Zari.

"Fine. I'll tell them to stop by and see you."

"They better. Now go on and fix you a plate and go

out back with your aunties nem'. You ain't come over here to sit inside and suck up all my AC."

Snickering, Keegan stood to her feet. "Love you, Granny, and thank you."

"Mhm, child. You just do what I told you. I'm not gon' be worrying about you and your mama hear?"

Keegan nodded. "Yes, ma'am."

After washing her hands, Keegan fixed her a plate of ribs, cabbage, mac n' cheese, corn on the cob and sweet potatoes before going out on the back porch. Her family sat around playing spades and dominoes while the music blasted. These were the days she missed as a little girl. No worries, no bills, no threats from people or nothing. Just surrounded by love and giving it right back. The only thing missing was the person who was assigned to love her first; Chrissy.

Five hours went by before Keegan decided to leave. Still in her feelings, she headed to the only place she knew she could relieve some stress. It'd been a minute since she hit up the casino, and for that reason alone was why she was even going.

Her hand itched as she walked through the entrance and headed straight for the craps table. She ordered a drink, the drink she always orders when feeling lucky, and took a seat. She stayed to herself, focusing on the game. Men had been sliding lustful looks her way all evening, but she ignored them. She wasn't here for entertainment unless it involved taking their money.

And, that she did. Five games later, she grabbed her chips and walked off with a smile on her face. She was up $20,000 and couldn't believe it. She'd hit it big before but that was after damn near staking out at the place.

"Fuck, yes," she cheered.

She couldn't believe she had hit for so much in such a short period of time but wasn't complaining. This was just what she needed to get started for school. A little down payment. To celebrate her win, she decided to grab a bottle of liquor on her way home and call her girls. She was sure Misani wouldn't have approved of her gambling, but hey! She'd come up nicely and didn't feel the urge to stay to make more.

After Keegan cashed in her chips, she headed straight to Big Lou's gas station. He was an OG in the hood she'd grown up in. With a pair of lethal hands that could lay any man on his back, Big Lou had gained a little fame from boxing. It wasn't until he received a concussion after he'd met his match that he stopped. Giving back to the hood that supported him and showed mad love, he opened up a gas station. When telling directions, anyone from KC would use it as a landmark of their location.

Pulling into the parking lot, Keegan grimaced seeing a bunch of dope boys posted out front. Not because she disliked any of them, hell she knew most of them, but because they always tried making a pass at her. Sighing, she parked and hopped out while locking her car.

"What up, Kee," one spoke giving her a head nod.

"Hey."

"Damn. You fine as hell, girl," another praised holding the door open for her. "What you doing tonight?"

Keegan chuckled. "Thanks and minding my business."

"Word? Shit, let me mind it too."

Shaking her head no and laughing, she ignored the guy and waved at Big Lou who was behind the counter. No matter how up in age he got, he was at his store almost every day. Knowing Envie probably wouldn't drink the hard liquor she was getting, she grabbed her a bottle of Raspberry Sangria Carlo Rossi before walking toward the counter.

"What's going on darling," Big Lou greeted.

"Hey. Nothing much. Can I get a fifth of Patron?"

"Is that it?"

Keegan nodded. "Mhm. Busy night?"

"It's not too bad. It'll pick up come tomorrow. Start of the weekend," he said, bagging her drinks up.

"Well, don't work too hard."

Big Lou smiled swiping her card. "I'll try not to."

Grabbing her bag, Keegan thanked him and headed

back outside. She was ready to turn up with her girls and relax. The same guy who held the door open for her was still shooting his shot and Keegan was amused. She had no issue with it, but her mind had been on Ramzi all week. Dealing with him brought something new into her life and she liked that. Nothing with him was a guessing game and Keegan felt like she could be herself around and with him.

"I see you drinking tonight. What's the occasion, ma?" the guy asked.

"Nothing special," she kept it brief continuing her stride, but stopped when she saw a woman who resembled her mother crossing the street.

Stuck dead in her tracks, Keegan watched as Chrissy basically played in traffic while looking a complete mess. When a car almost hit her, Keegan gasped in utter panic. Her heart beat erratically as Chrissy skipped along laughing as if she hadn't been seconds away from losing her life. She toyed with death as if it meant nothing to her.

"Damn," the guy vying for Keegan's attention yelled. "That bitch almost got smacked by that SUV."

"Come on, man. Don't call the lady out her name," his boy said.

"She a fucking dopehead. You already know she coming to see us."

Keegan heard everything they were saying, but her

eyes were on her mother. Clothes, hair and mind disheveled, Chrissy was high as a kite and felt free as ever. She'd thinned out so much, her jaws were sunken in and the already size zero clothes were baggy on her frame. Keegan gulped as a wave of nausea settled in the pit of her stomach, before quickly traveling up her chest. She pinched her lips to keep her vomit down and blinked away her tears. Just as Chrissy was about to walk by her, Keegan called her name.

"Ma," she called out hoarsely.

"Oh, shit. That's her mama," one of the guys whispered.

Keegan cleared her throat and spoke louder. "Mama!"

Chrissy spun around at the hiss in the girl's voice and she blinked quickly before smiling. She didn't recognize her own daughter at first and Keegan knew it.

"Oh, hey. Hey, girl," Chrissy said jovially. "What's going on?"

"Ma, it's me; Keegan."

Chrissy grinned, chapped lips peeling in the process. "I know who you are. You got that for me?"

A stab of guilt lay buried in her chest at her mother's words. "Come talk to me over here right quick."

"I'll be right back," she told the group of guys.

Keegan didn't bother to look back to see if Chrissy was following her; she knew she would. The mere thought of

Keegan having whatever drug Chrissy was in search of had her damn near sprinting to her vehicle in the worn-down chucks on her feet. She'd just gotten high no more than twenty minutes ago and was zooted. Knowing she'd be coming down soon, she needed to score again.

"This your ride?" Chrissy asked, running her hand over the hood of Keegan's Benz. Her eyes grew wide with excitement. "This shit is clean. I could get so much money off this."

She was talking to herself. Scheming on her own daughter and didn't seem to mind if Keegan heard her at all. Keegan swallowed the aching sob that rose in her throat.

"Where have you been?" she asked in a concerned tone. "I've been looking for you."

"You ain't been looking hard enough. I'm everywhere I should be at."

"No," Keegan hissed. "You're out here in these streets costing people their lives. Look at you!"

Chrissy fanned a hand down the front of her body. "Look at me! I'm fine Keegan. What you call me over here for?"

"I want you to get help," she damn near cried. "You almost got me and you killed. Why'd you rob that guy?"

Keegan whispered that; not wanting others to hear her. She had plans to sit inside her car and talk to Chrissy, but with the way her eyes lit up just at the outside Keegan wouldn't be surprised if she stole something from her from the inside.

"I don't know what you're talking about. I ain't rob nobody."

"Where have you been staying? Are you safe?"

Chrissy chuckled. "Like you care. You don't give a fuck about me. Your own mama. I raised you and you wanna turn your back on me like I ain't shit. Yeah! I do drugs, but so what daughter? The shit makes me feel good. It makes me feel freeee," she sang and began to skip around the pavement.

Keegan's heart squeezed in anguish as she realized there was no hope for her mother. Having gone months without laying eyes on her, it wasn't until now that Keegan felt the effects of her drug abuse shattering. Chrissy simply didn't care. As long as she was high, there wasn't shit anyone, even her own child, could tell her. Keegan took deep inhales until she felt like she was good to speak.

"I just want you better and off this shit. You don't even look the same," Keegan pleaded.

"People age all the time. You gotta stop worrying so much about me and focus on you. This my life Keegan. I'ma do whatever makes me happy."

It sounded as if Keegan's granny had spoken for her

daughter. She'd told her the same thing hours before and Keegan guessed it was what she needed to abide by. The more she stuck her neck out for Chrissy, placing her heart on the line, she was going to end up hurt or worse. She'd already been caught up once and not many times were second chances given.

"Is that what you really want me to do?" Keegan asked.

"Do whatever you want but leave me the hell out of it," Chrissy spat, turning away from her and walked toward the dope boys.

Keegan's hands trembled, struggling to hold onto her bag. Her eyes filled with tears as she unlocked her car, climbed inside and watched the same guy who was trying to shoot his shot sell her mother drugs. It was a horror movie in live-action the way fear gripped her. Dead or alive, the drugs were killing Chrissy and Keegan didn't want to think the next time she'd hear from her would be from a morgue, but she couldn't help but to.

Her eyes stayed trained on her until she disappeared down the block. Keegan wanted to follow her, but her granny's words echoed loudly in her ear.

"I want to save you, but I have to save myself," she said aloud wiping the tear from her cheek.

The plan to call her girls up quickly changed. Keegan wanted to be alone, well she did at first. After peeling the seal to her bottle of Patron and drinking straight from it while driving, she thought of Ramzi. She needed to see him. She needed his calmness to blanket her erratic thoughts and wounded soul. It was beyond reckless for her to drink and drive but Keegan wasn't thinking clearly. After she ran through a red light, she sobered up a bit and pulled over into a parking lot.

Tossing her car in park, her glossed eyes stared straight ahead at nothing in particular and she burst into tears. Sobbing, she cradled her phone in her hand and dialed Ramzi's number with blurred vision.

"Gorgeous," he answered warmly. "What's going on?"

"C-Can you come get me," she heaved.

Inside his office at Façade, Ramzi sat up in his chair and turned the volume on his phone down. He had a few people in there with him. Telling them to give him a minute, he waited until they left out and the door was shut to speak.

"Where you at Keegan?"

"I'm drunk," she whined, sniffling.

"Okay, baby. Just tell me where you at though. I'ma come get you," he said, snatching his gun out of his safe and grabbing his keys.

Keegan looked around, trying to locate where she had parked at. Thankfully, it was in the parking lot of a grocery store with a well-lit up lot and cameras. Still, she was drunk and not in her right mind to be out like that by herself.

"I'm at Jewel's," she told him.

"A'ight. I'm on the way. Your doors locked?"

She nodded and wiped at her eyes.

"Keegan, are your doors locked?" Ramzi repeated.

"Yes. No one's gonna get me," she giggled. "They might though. Remember how those men kidnapped me? They're probably still looking for me."

"No one is looking for you," he sighed, pulling out of the back parking lot. "Why you drinking and driving, ma? You know that shit is dangerous and against the law."

"I'm sad. Well I wasn't sad until I saw my mama. I finally get to lay eyes on her and she basically told me to leave her the hell alone." She started crying again and Ramzi shook his head.

He'd never been around Keegan drunk and he didn't mind it because everyone had their issues, but he had to prepare himself. She was an emotional drinker anyway and the shit with Chrissy didn't make her situation any better. Ramzi just listened to her cries until she calmed down.

"Why doesn't she love me enough to get clean? What did I do to her?" she sniveled, needing answers.

The pain laced through her words formed a knot in

his stomach as he hiked his speed limit. He had to get to her.

"You didn't do anything, baby. Sometimes the people we put so much faith in to do the right thing just don't. It's not that she doesn't love you enough; she doesn't love herself enough. You can do everything for a person and if it's not enough to them, it'll never be enough and you have to be okay with that."

"But I don't wanna be okay with that though," she breathed. "She needs help."

Keegan hated how her heart felt. It was heavy and aching, causing her breaths to quicken. When she went to pick up the bottle, she stopped and shook her head. She knew the signs of an addict. They started small and increased before you could get a handle on them. Keegan didn't want to cope by using alcohol now that she'd slowed down on gambling. The bottle was about empty anyway. Once the Patron began to taste like whatever, she'd kept sipping.

"How close are you?" she sighed just wanting Ramzi near her already.

"I'm pulling in now."

Parking his car behind hers, Ramzi hopped out leaving it running. Keegan hit her locks and he opened her door. Thankfully, she had on a seatbelt while being reckless. Unbuckling it, he pulled her out of the seat and into his embrace. Keegan thought she was all cried out, but the minute she was in his arms she cried silent tears.

"It hurts so bad," she told him.

He knew it did. Her pain was undeniable. "I know ma. Get it all out."

Feeling protected enough to let more of her guards down, Keegan let Ramzi console her while she promised to shed her last tears over Chrissy. It was more painful to be denied and turned down than it was knowing her mother was out using. Keegan was defeated. She once felt trapped knowing she had an obligation to look after Chrissy but not anymore. As free as Chrissy said she was, Keegan was as well.

Inhaling a few breaths, she pulled away from him but he didn't let her go. Without pity in his eyes, Ramzi wiped her cheeks and pecked her lips.

"Feel better?"

"A little bit. My head is killing me," she groaned.

Ramzi chuckled. "I bet it is. Wait until the morning."

She groaned and hugged him again. "Thank you. You really don't know how much I appreciate you."

"I'm glad you called me. I woulda been fucked up had something happened to you."

"I was tripping. I should be good now though."

Ramzi shook his head no with a smirk. "Don't even try

to play that. I'm not letting you drive home tonight, so come get in my car."

"You're taking me to your house?" she asked as he guided her to the passenger side and opened the door.

"Yep. Unless you got somewhere else you trying to go?"

She shook her head. "No. With you is the only place I want to be."

Glossy-eyed and in her feelings, Keegan looked upward at him and her heart expanded. Ramzi was so calm and collected. The type of man who played no games about the woman he was pursuing nor had time to. Keegan didn't want to say she was falling in love with him, but she was falling in something, that was for sure. She just hoped her baggage wasn't too heavy to tug along and unpack because she had plenty of it. Good thing Ramzi liked taking trips. He was well-prepared and equipped to accommodate any luggage with her. As long as she'd let him help her unpack what was inside, he'd always carry the load.

After grabbing her things from her car and locking it up, Ramzi asked her if it was okay if his cousin came to pick her car up. Keegan let him know it was and they pulled out the lot. On the drive to his place, they sat in silence. Keegan was in an alcoholic daze staring at the city as they passed it by. Grabbing her hand, Ramzi gave it a squeeze.

"You good?"

"Yeah. Trying not to fall asleep," she chuckled. "I drank way too much."

Ramzi smirked still holding her hand. "For a reason. What else you do tonight?"

"I went to the casino after I left my granny's house."

"You win something?"

"Mhm," she grinned. "Twenty."

His eyes shot over to hers in amusement. "Twenty what?"

"Twenty thousand," she laughed. "Why're you looking like that?"

"I wasn't expecting you to say that. You must really know what you doing hitting like that."

Keegan shrugged. Feeling it was a better time than any, she let him know about the slight gambling addiction she had been doing good at shaking until today.

"Yeah. Honestly, I used to gamble a lot. It was how I coped and made money when I was younger. My mama has been on drugs for a while now but I didn't think it was this bad until I was snatched up. It's something I've started to quit doing but tonight made me really not want to anymore. An addiction is an addiction no matter the vice.

Ramzi had to agree. He hadn't personally fallen victim to addiction but witnessed it and Keegan was right.

"Why you didn't say anything when we went to Vegas?"

"I didn't want to ruin our trip. That's why I let you do most of it. I wasn't trying to fall into the deep end because I know how downhill it can go for me."

"Damn," he sighed. "I wish you would've told me."

"Don't feel bad. I should've said something."

"I know now though. What else is a trigger?"

Keegan shook her head. "Nothing really. Those were my two go-to favorites. When I was younger, I used to shoot dice, play pool, make bets on games and all," she chuckled. "It was ridiculous."

"You bought scratch-offs too, huh?" he joked and Keegan nodded with a smile.

"Yep. They used to piss me off when I didn't win shit, so I stopped. What's your vice? You have a weakness I should know about?"

"You."

"Me?" Keegan whispered.

Ramzi nodded. "Yeah. From the first day we ran into each other you had my head gone. That's just real shit. Something about you intrigued me. Your eyes gave you away. Like you were holding so much in and I wanted to know. I had to get to know you. I just wanted to be around you."

Keegan gulped. "Wow. I um...I honestly didn't know you felt like that. I mean, I knew you liked me but sheesh."

They chuckled.

"Yeah, it's that deep."

"Is that a bad thing? You know too much of something is never good," she told him.

"Too much of something like what? You?" He chuckled lowly. "Nah. I don't think I'll ever get enough of you."

Keegan wanted to fan herself but the air was already blowing. Ramzi wasn't holding back tonight. Instead of fanning herself like she wanted to do, she tucked her hands between her legs. His words had all the liquor traveling from her belly directly to her clitoris. It was thumping as if it'd been drinking and had a vicious headache.

Not knowing what to say, Keegan sat quietly, just absorbing the energy Ramzi gave off. Being in his presence was enough for her; sometimes words didn't need to be shared. Plus, the words he'd just spoken could hold her over for a while. They were what she needed to hear when she needed to hear them.

When they finally made it to his crib, Keegan had

fallen asleep. Ramzi knew he could've carried her inside on some fairytale shit, but she'd been drinking and was going to be nothing but dead weight. Plus, he wanted to let her know they'd arrived so she could assess her surroundings. Though she let him come pick her up, Ramzi wanted her to be well aware of where she was.

Once awake, Keegan yawned and grabbed his hand that was held out to help her up. The light in the garage provided them a pathway that led inside the house. Inside, Keegan fidgeted, eyes dancing around the spacious living room.

"Where's your bathroom?"

"There's one right here; come on."

Walking through the living room, they stepped inside the kitchen that had a restroom attached to it. Scurrying toward it, Keegan told him thank you and that she'd be right out. Popping his neck and the days stress away, Ramzi pulled his cell phone from his pocket and opened up his text thread. While Keegan was out of sight, he wanted to get this done. He'd been thinking about it the entire ride.

Shooting a text to his homegirl who had connections in high places, thanks to her father, he let her know he needed a favor. It was a simple one really; one that he hoped helped her in the long run.

CHAPTER SEVEN

"Everything with your lawyer turned out good, right?" Zeek asked his daughter over the phone.

The two had stayed in contact, more so of Zeek reaching out to Zari than the other way around. He didn't mind though. He was determined to show and prove to her that he wanted to be in her life.

"Yes. He had no choice but to come up off that money. I wasn't having it any other way."

Zeek smirked. "I bet. You still coming over for Labor Day? I'm throwing some food on the grill."

"Who's all going to be there?" Zari asked as she turned onto her cousin Jhalil's block.

"Just a few friends and some family members. It's been years since they saw you so I hope you can come out."

Zari chewed on the inside of her jaw in contemplation. She didn't want to be rude and decline his offer but
being around a bunch of folks who more than likely had
her name in their mouth without her being in their presence wasn't her thing.

"I don't know," she told him sucking her teeth when
she saw Flip's car. "I'll let you know. I had plans that day,
but they may change."

"Alright. Just let me know. I didn't want anything
though. Just calling to check on you," he said meaning it.

"Oh okay. Well I'll talk to you later."

Zeek told her okay and they hung up. Parking next to
her cousin Jaci's car, Zari shut her car off and climbed out.
She wasn't expecting to see Flip over Jhalil's place and
wished Jaci would've given her a heads up. Then again,
she had no clue the two weren't on good terms. Zari had
slid through to drop off a couple pairs of heels and a
designer bag Jaci asked could she have. With as much shit
as she had in her closet, Zari didn't mind giving her cousin
whatever even though she knew she could buy it more
than once with her income.

Ringing the doorbell, she waited patiently for one of
them to open up. She prayed it wasn't Flip and thankfully
it wasn't. Jhalil's fiancée Carmen pulled the door open
and smiled.

"Hey Zari. Come in girl."

"That ring gets bigger every time I see it," Zari joked as they hugged.

"You think so? Don't let your cousin hear that," she snickered. "How've you been?"

"Good, girl. Just stopped by to see Jaci and that big head fiancé of yours. I see he has company."

Carmen led her to the living room where everyone was. "Mhm. Your boo," she grinned.

"That ain't no boo of mine," she mumbled, but wanted to take her words back when her eyes landed on him.

Flip had his eyes on the TV but glanced to his right when they walked in. He looked Zari over and she didn't miss the sparkle in his eyes. Yeah, she looked damn good that day and for a good reason. She'd just gotten paid out of the ass yesterday thanks to Maverick's reckless behavior and today she had celebrated all by herself.

High-waisted overly distressed boyfriend jeans covered a sleeveless red one-piece top that had her boobs spilling out. Her hair was in a long ponytail with choppy bangs giving her an exotic look and of course, a pair of heels were on her feet. Diamonds iced her neck, ears and wrist out and Flip couldn't help but notice the Chanel bag he'd copped her draped over her shoulder. She winked in his direction and poked her lips out in a 'Yeah, nigga. You see me' kind of way.

Zari peeped him too though. Fresh locs were twisted

neatly to the back of his head in a fancy design, while he rocked a Billionaire Boys Club tee, jean shorts and colored Air Max Plus shoes. He wasn't sporting any jewelry but didn't need to. He was chilling.

"What up cuz," Jhalil spoke, pulling Zari into a hug.

"Hey. What y'all got going on over here?"

Jhalil flopped down on the couch next to Carmen. "Shit. Chilling, about to grab some food in a minute."

"I thought you wanted me to cook?" Carmen asked him.

"Nah. We can go pick something up. I need to run to the bank anyway."

While they had their own conversation, Zari stared Flip upside his head. His attention was back on the TV and she had the right mind to mush his ass but was trying to keep her hands to herself. Instead, she sucked her teeth.

"You don't see me standing here?" she sassed.

Flip slowly looked her way. "Yo daddy wasn't a glass-maker, was he?"

Jhalil couldn't help but laugh, pissing Zari off even more. She tossed him the bird and verbally cursed at Flip.

"Fuck you," she huffed, heading out of the living room to find the person she came to see.

Carmen giggled. "What's up with y'all?"

"I don't even know anymore to be honest."

"Better get that taken care of," Jhalil told him. "You know how she gets when she doesn't get her way."

"I ain't near worried about it. She spoiled as fuck and that's the issue right there."

Flip wasn't stunting Zari and her attitude. She could've easily spoken to him like she'd done Jhalil, but of course she had to be stubborn. Flip was going to let her be too. Clearly, she hadn't gotten her mind right yet.

Stomping into the spare bedroom she knew her cousin would be in, Zari pushed the door open. Propped up on the bed with her boo on FaceTime, Jaci waved her cousin inside.

"Babe, let me call you back. My cousin just got here," she told him.

"A'ight. Don't be faking either."

Jaci smirked. "I won't. Promise."

Smiling, she plugged her phone back into the charger and set it on the dresser. "What's up, hoe? I didn't know you were here."

"You would've known had you not been back here cup caking. Who was that?" Zari asked, setting her purse on the bed and handing Jaci the bag of goodies she'd brought.

"This one guy I've been seeing. He's not in the streets; can you believe that?"

The two laughed and honestly Zari couldn't. Jaci had

grown up whipping work for Jhalil and Flip at a young age. It was her side hustle while in school to become a pharmacist and boy had it paid off. She was living the life she'd always dreamed of. The only thing missing was a few babies running around, but she was giving herself at least another five years before she planned to pop any out.

Between her and Zari, they gave Jhalil gray hairs before he was intended to grow them. With him being in the streets, they figured dating a guy just like him wasn't bad. Jaci learned the hard way and Zari learned to date whoever had the fattest pockets and was giving the money up. Street nigga or not; she'd learned her lesson too. Men were all trash in her book.

"I can. You all sophisticated and whatnot. You need you a square to keep you balanced," Zari laughed.

"Whatever. You already know I can take it there if it comes down to it. I was ready to beat that ballplayer's ass. Him and his fiancée. I don't play about you; you know that."

It took every bit of convincing for Jhalil to not have Maverick knocked off. He could've had it done that next night, but Zari begged him not to. With their altercation having gone viral, Zari didn't want any of her family to be interrogated by the law. She was sure they'd take Maverick's side.

"I know. I'm just messing with you. Do those Jimmy

Choo's fit? Those hoes almost gave me a corn on my pinky toe," she fussed.

Jaci stood from the bed and wiggled her ankle from side to side. "Oooh, yes. These are fly. I'm so glad we wear the same size. Let me see what else is in here. I may have to step out tonight."

"Yeah, right. You don't be going two places. I invited you to the bar with me that one night and your ass never texted me back."

"Girl, I fell asleep. I be needing a nap before I go out now. Does that make me old?" she chuckled.

"Nope. But you missed out on some money. You are still single and there were plenty of sugar daddies at the bar that night."

Jaci frowned and shook her head. She had nothing against the way her cousin made her money, or used to rather, but she couldn't do it. Regardless of Zari not having sex with the men she dated, Jaci knew that somewhere in their minds, sex would be brought up. She just couldn't wrap her mind around it all but gave kudos to Zari. She was so player with her game.

"I'm not interested in no dang sugar daddy, cousin. And you shouldn't be either. Not anymore. I thought you and Flip were making progress? I asked about you when I got here and he straight ignored my ass," she chuckled, sliding on another pair of heels.

Zari rolled her eyes. She couldn't stand his fine chocolate self. After giving her a brief rundown of why they were at odds, Jaci stared blankly at her.

"What!?" Zari screeched in only the dramatic way she could. "Am I wrong?"

"No, not necessarily wrong completely, but you are a little bit."

She huffed. "I swear, you and Misani never have a bitch back. I'm the one hurting here, not him."

"You don't know that. Let me explain it to you like this. You see how your daddy is trying to come back into your life? You give him a chance, he's on his shit for a while being the best father ever, earning your trust, you're enjoying the bond y'all are building, and then all of a sudden, he disappears again. When you ask what happened or why, he tells you he thought he was ready to be in your life, but now he's not."

"I wish his ass would," Zari hissed.

"See! It's the same thing with you and Flip. You've been leading and dragging this man on for years. The minute he says he wants commitment; you clam up with no real explanation other than you're not ready yet."

"But I am," she whined. "Kind of. I just don't want it to turn into a relationship like the one with Zeek. Yeah, Flip has been around for years, but so was Zeek before he just dipped out. I'm not putting up with that again."

Zari couldn't focus on her present relationships because she was still trying to take care of the little girl in her. The one who hadn't been showed what real love was like. The one who wished she had a father to protect her from the evils and demons of the world. It was a struggle to even let Zeek this close to her, especially since he wasn't dishing out money.

Once that thought entered her mind, she relaxed some on the bed. If she was in constant contact with any man, there was business being discussed. It was all so new to her for Zeek to be calling just to check up on her, but Flip had done that for years. He didn't have to spend a dime on Zari for her to fuck with him and they both knew that. The only thing was, Zari didn't know how to express herself and let him know that.

"And you don't have to but come on Zari. The man loves you; that's a no brainer."

"And what exactly am I supposed to do with love when I can't even reciprocate that shit?" Zari asked, leaving Jaci stumped.

"That my girl is something you'll have to ask yourself. I wish I could give you the answer, but only you know how your heart feels when it comes to him. My advice would be to take a chance. Who knows what could happen?"

Pondering over her words, Zari promised to put some

action behind them. The two caught up on the latest family gossip and planned to link up for lunch or dinner sometime next week. When they were walking out of the bedroom, Flip was walking down the hall. His tall frame sauntered with a swag that Zari couldn't miss.

"Y'all headed out? We was about to grab something to eat," he told them.

"Yeah. I got some errands to run," Jaci answered.

She hugged him around the waist and whispered, "Don't be mean. See you later cousin. Love you."

"Love you too," Zari told her.

Flip looked Zari over and turned back around.

"Flip, wait," Zari breathed out. He turned around to face her.

"What up?"

"Can I talk to you for a minute? It won't take long."

He nodded his head once and Zari sighed with content. She hadn't had to argue with him about speaking to her so that was good. That meant they were off to a good start. Stepping back inside the bedroom, Flip entered behind her and shut the door. He stood there while Zari ambled over to the dresser and leaned against it.

Drinking him in, she smiled to herself at how fine he was. From that night in his car when they first met, she knew she was going to fuck him. Never did she think fucking would turn into falling in love. She cringed a bit just thinking of how that sounded, but her stomach fluttered as well. The mixture of emotions she was feeling for this man was deepening by the day and she couldn't stop them if she tried.

"Your ass ain't this quiet. Talk," he told her and Zari sucked her teeth.

"See. Why you gotta talk to me like that? I'm trying to have a civil conversation."

"Zari," he said slowly and she rolled her eyes.

"Fine whatever. I wanted to tell you that I thought about what you said and I'm ready."

Flip reached under his shirt and scratched at his stomach. "Ready for what?"

Sidetracked by his simple action, Zari blinked her eyes a few times trying not to let lust and the fact that she hadn't had dick in weeks cloud her judgment.

"Man, I ain't doing this shit with you," Flip said, snapping her back into reality.

"Wait, nigga. Damn. You the one threw me off lifting your shirt all up. I'm trying to stay focused."

"Like you ain't got yo titties all out. If you just called me in here to fuck, say that."

She frowned but her pussy pulsed at his slick words. "What? No, that's not why. I mean, but we can."

Flip smirked and shook his head. "What you gotta say to me girl?"

Putting her pride to the side for the sake of not wanting to ever be done with him, Zari let him know how she really felt. All week she'd been going back and forth with herself about what'd she say to him when the time came. The time had presented itself and she decided to keep it real with him. He deserved that.

"It was hard for me to tell you I love you because I don't even know what that means. As crazy as I may sound, I allowed myself to love you but only so much. I gave myself to you on my terms, in bits and pieces, because I didn't want you to hurt me like other men in my life have. I was protecting me not realizing you were doing the same."

Flip had a surprising look on his face. He wasn't expecting her to get right to the issue but was proud of her for owning up to it.

"I know I can let my guard down with you. I know that, but sometimes I get scared. As long as I have control of any situation I'm in, I can control the outcome. Well, that's what I thought," she said rolling her eyes. "I can't control how my heart beats for you. It's weird but I've been accepting it for a while but ignoring it too. So, that's that. I guess what I'm trying to say is I want to be with you. I'm sorry for flaunting these men in your face, especially that stunt I pulled at the club."

"Damn right," he boasted.

"Can I finish?" she said and they chuckled. "I'm ready to put this lifestyle behind me and start a new one. With you... exclusively. No more dating apps, date nights, flights out of town, expensive gifts, sending nude pictures."

"A'ight, man," he groaned stopping her. "I get it. I hear you baby and I appreciate you for being mature enough to point out your wrongs. Was there anything you want me to change since we're turning over a new leaf?"

Zari smiled and shook her head. Walking over to him, she wrapped her arms around his neck and kissed his chin. "Nope. I love you just the way you are. Thank you for making me realize how selfish I was being. I didn't know you felt that way until you said something."

"Yeah. Had been, but I was letting you do your thing. That's what seemed to make you happy, so why try and come in between that you know?"

"You make me happy too," she cooed rubbing her hands up his chest. "You really do Alphonso. Sorry for not letting you know how I really felt."

He kissed her forehead. "It's all good, ma. We on the same page now, so that's all that matters."

"Since we're making up, can I get some dick?" she

asked boldly. "You been holding out, depriving me of what I thought belonged to me."

Flip licked his lips as she undid his belt and unbuttoned his jean shorts. "It does belong to you. But you knew that. Gon' remind me of what I've been missing."

"Gladly," she purred while lowering into a squatting position.

"Take them tight ass jeans off."

"No. It took me too long to get in them. Let me get you off and we can worry about me later."

His brow lifted. "Word? You must really be sorry."

She yanked his boxers down and fisted his semi-erection. "Shut up."

Teasing the tip of his dick with her tongue, she swirled it around getting herself reacquainted with it. The harder and longer he grew, the wetter Zari's mouth got. Her nipples stung when she inhaled him into her warm mouth and Flip hissed, grabbing ahold of her ponytail.

"Shit."

Sloppily, she sucked him off showing her gratitude for his patience. Deepthroating him, Zari looked up and hummed along his pole. Flip's chest heaved and eye twitched. Zari's head game was lethal. Pulling back slowly, she got a rhythm going and sucked him just how he liked. Slow and steady for a few was his thing before Zari picked up her pace.

"Fuck my face, baby," she managed to tell him in between slurps.

Grabbing the front of her throat and back of her head, Flip did as he was told. Stretching her mouth wide, his dick pounded into her wet mouth. Suctioning him with each stroke, Flip felt his balls tighten. His bottom lip was tucked in his mouth and eyes stuck in the back of his head. Letting her breathe for a minute, he pulled out and Zari puckered her lips. He slapped it against them a few times before she began to jack him off.

"Mmm. That dick tastes so good. It's mine?"

Flip nodded. He couldn't speak. Zari smiled and slid her mouth back over him. This time she took control. Using both hands she sucked him off and rotated her hands around his length. The hold he had on her freshly done ponytail didn't deter Zari from her mission. He could've snatched the bitch smooth from her head and she wouldn't have cared. Knowing he'd pay to get it fixed, she sucked faster. Harder. Nastier.

"Shit!" he grunted, feeling his nut approaching.

Keeping the pace, Zari looked him in the eyes and snatched his soul from his body. Gripping her head with both hands, he moaned lowly while his seeds traveled down the back of her throat. He held her there for seconds after he'd released trying to catch his breath. Zari tapped his leg and pushed him back some.

"Damn. My bad baby," he apologized hoarsely.

Zari snickered. "Trying to kill me. I mean I could breathe, but only for so long."

Taking a seat on the carpet, Zari exhaled loudly and licked her lips. Untying the heels she had on, she tossed them to the side and unbuttoned her jeans before unzipping them.

"What'chu doing?"

"Help me take these off. I need some dick right now. I'm not waiting until later."

He licked his lips and shook his head. "I'm not fucking you in this man's crib. We can just go to the car right quick."

"I don't wanna go to the car," she pouted and Flip shook his head again.

"Well, you ain't getting no dick then. Either we do that or wait until after we get some food."

Zari rolled her eyes. "Fine. Where we 'bout to eat at?"

They stared at each other before cracking up laughing. She sounded just like the little boy who'd gone viral for saying that. Putting her heels back on, she refastened her jeans and Flip helped her up. Pulling her into his chest, he tongued her down and squeezed on her booty.

"I love you Zariella," he told her, kissing along her neck.

She moaned softly. "I love you too Alphonso."

"How much?"

"Enough to suck that dick of yours in another woman's house," she laughed. "Let's go to the car, babe. I'm too horny to wait."

Flip smirked. "That's what I thought."

"Oh, wait. I forgot to tell you. I got my money yesterday."

"From ol' boy?"

Zari nodded and smiled. "Yep. So, where you wanna go for your birthday that's in a few weeks? You get an all-expenses-paid vacation."

"I'm not picky, ma. Choose a place and book that shit. I'm happy as fuck for you, though. Bet that nigga keep his hands to himself next time. Wonder if I can still get him knocked-off."

Flip had been the one to make Zari get her passport, so he was sure she was picking a vacation spot out of the country. Back when things between them hadn't progressed yet, he told her since these men wanted to take her on dates, she needed to be prepared if one wanted to fly her out of the country.

Zari smacked his arm. "No. We're good. Shit, better than good for a while. Let's not focus on the past; just right now."

"Yeah, we can do that. I'm liking this new positive vibe you got going on."

Zari laughed as he opened the door and they walked out. "Enjoy it while it lasts. Knowing you, you'll do something to end all that shit."

Snatching her back to him around her waist, she giggled and fell into his chest. A place she'd always felt comfortable being. Flip was more than her protector. He was her lover and friend as well. Zari cherished their relationship and made a vow to not let anyone or anything come between them.

$$$

I nside of Carlo's large bathroom, Misani stood in nothing but her bra and panties while brushing her teeth. On a Saturday afternoon just waking up from their mid-day nap, she couldn't help but smile. Since the night they picked Marisa up, things between she and Carlo had only progressed. Misani had basically been off the grid and out of the way for the most part, with Carlo not far behind.

With their relationship built off trust, he picked up an insatiable need to be in her presence. He loved her vibe and they seemed to vibe even better these days now that they had cleared the air. She was comfortable around him and had opened up much more about her past. When she told him what she and Zari had been through, Carlo found even more respect for her.

Misani was a hustler straight out the mud. However she could get it, she got it. Whatever needed to be done to provide for hers, she was making a way. What she didn't play with was her money or her family. For them, she'd go to war with whomever.

Rinsing her mouth out, she smiled lazily in the mirror at Carlo walking in behind her. His smooth caramel skin looked yummy with nothing covering it except a pair of boxers. Those pensive brown eyes stared back at her as he stood directly behind her. His large dick pressing firmly against her ass cheeks made Misani squirm.

Carlo kissed along her shoulder. "You trembling already and I haven't done anything yet."

That voice. Gosh! Misani still wanted to record every conversation they had just so she could play it back during any time of the day. He didn't try to have a sexy bedroom voice; he just did. His trimmed goatee brushed against her shoulder as his lips reached her neck.

"Skin so damn soft," he rasped, sliding his hands between her legs.

"Carlo," she moaned. "We're going to be late."

"Hush and bend over."

His command was met by an eager Misani who obliged without protest. Putting an arch in her back, she exhaled as he kissed across her shoulder blades and left a wet trail with his tongue down her spine. He gripped her barely-there love handles, sliding her boy shorts down her legs. Kissing each cheek, he spread them before dragging his tongue from the front of her soaked kitty, to the top of her crack. Needing to really taste her, Carlo spun her around and lifted her with ease onto the sink.

"Oohh!" Misani gasped, as he spread her lips and nastily sucked her clit into his mouth.

The cool countertop against her cheeks and his warm mouth on her brought an indescribable feeling. The tip of his tongue flicked with determination over her bud, making it harder and her center slicker. She was leaking like crazy already and that just let him know she was already wet for him.

While he played in her wetness, he tugged his boxers down, kicking them to the side. Stroking himself, he kept eating as Misani palmed his head. His soft, textured hair slid through her fingers as she tried her best to grip something. He was licking her too good. Too fast. Too skillfully and she was losing it.

"B-Bae! You gon' make me come!" she moaned loudly.

Carlo wasn't about to torture his girl. He needed her to come in his mouth within the next ten seconds flat. He wrapped his plump lips around her swollen clit, showing her no mercy. Sticking his tongue in her gooiness, he used his thumb to rub her clit. The lubrication from her wetness was all he needed.

"D'Carlooo!" she shouted. Stomach caving in as her orgasm reached its peak.

He went back to flicking her clit across the most sensitive part and Misani came undone.

"Mhm," Carlo smacked his lips and kept licking. "Gimmie that shit, bae."

Misani's body sat completely up on the counter as she came hard, squirting her juices all over him and the floor. Her frame continued to tremble as he made sure every drop, the ones he could lick up, was in his mouth. Misani had what Carlo considered rich pussy. The shit tasted exquisite. Expensive. Well-crafted and was made specifically for him. He'd be a fool not to cherish it.

Carlo kissed her vagina once more and lifted up. Her legs twitched and pussy jumped when he came up to kiss her. Sliding his palm over her slick folds, he rubbed the juices along his dick and stroked it while making Misani taste herself. Pulling her closer to him, Carlo palmed her booty as she sucked on his tongue. He played at the entrance of her treasure and Misani spread her legs more for him.

"Put it in, daddy," she moaned against his ear and lost her breath once he slid smoothly inside of her.

Carlo breathed hard. Her warmth, tight, wetness

wrapped around him in a chokehold. He wanted to lift his head from her shoulder and look in her eyes, those weird sexy colored eyes of hers, but he had to focus. If not, he was going to be releasing in seconds. Once he was able to calm down, Misani swirled her hips in a slow manner, fucking him slowly from her position.

"Your shit is so wet," he groaned, watching her leak onto him. Marking her territory yet again.

"You make me this way," she whined as he dug deeper.

Holding him around the neck, Carlo picked her up and slammed her up and down on his dick. His balls smacked against her cheeks with each thrust and the sound alone had him ready to bust. Misani panted loudly, tightening her walls around him.

"Fuck!" he shouted as his legs locked, balls tightened and nut shot out of him.

Holding tightly onto her with one arm, he snatched his dick from her center, gripped his dick and released on her exposed flesh. He came for what seemed like forever and Misani was turned on all over again at the feel of his hot sperm on her.

He placed her on her feet and chuckled. "Damn, girl."

Misani smiled and wiped the sweat from his forehead. "I know. Just what I needed."

"Says the person who cared about us being late."

She giggled and licked his bottom lip before sucking it into her mouth. "What time should I be ready again?"

"We got a good hour tops. You think you can be dressed by then?"

She nodded and clasped her hands around his wrists. He was pinching her nipples and they had no time to go another round, so she stopped him.

"If you give me some privacy and stop touching on me, I can be," she smiled softly.

"A'ight. Give me a kiss and I'll leave you alone."

Blushing, she pressed her lips against his. Carlo's hand found the back of her neck and he deepened it, wanting to show her just how much he enjoyed the feel of her. All of her. Breaking free, Misani struggled to catch her breath. Carlo just stared at her, taking in her flawless beauty.

Her hair sat atop her head in a messy bun, while her baby hairs swirled softly along her sweated-out edges. Her eyes rested lustfully low and Carlo smirked at the after-sex glow melting over her frame.

"What?" she asked softly.

"Nothing. You're just fine as hell, baby. It's hard to keep my eyes off you, for real."

She giggled and shooed him away. "Thank you, now get out before we don't make it."

Carlo smacked her booty as she bent down to pick up

a few things that fell on the ground. "A'ight. I'ma shower in the guest room."

"Okay. Want me to pick out your outfit?"

Carlo stopped at the door and smirked. "That's what we're doing now?"

"I mean yeah. Is that a problem? I'm probably the coldest dressed woman you've ever been with, baby," she flexed.

"Nah, you got that. I can't even front. Do your thang," he gave her the go-ahead to get him fly. Ultimately the goal was to match hers and Misani couldn't wait. Carlo wasn't a big fashion label dresser, but he had his pieces. Niggas couldn't out dress him on a bummy day.

Out of her shower, Misani oiled her body down in a light coat of shea butter before doing her facial routine. Slipping her undergarments on, she then slid into the orange snake print material bodysuit from *MAG Co.* The fabric was breathable and off the shoulders, so she paired it with a leather skirt and her favorite heels to date. The orange Money Motif pumps with a metal $ for a heel were to die for and so comfortable.

Once she was dressed, Misani did a natural look for her face and added a bold, matte red lipstick to make everything pop though it wasn't needed. She loved how it looked though. Fanning her lashes, she added some eyeliner before doing her brows. Pulling her hair into a neat topknot bun, she laid her baby hairs and put on some gold oversized earrings that made a huge statement. Puckering her lips in the mirror, she smiled and headed out to the bedroom.

Already dressed, Carlo equally matched her fly in a two-tone colored Karl Kani tee with orange embroidery, blue stoned washed jeans and some Air Max 98's on. He stood from the bed and let out a whistle.

"Shit."

"You like?" she smiled, doing a twirl.

"Hell yeah. Your legs in that skirt and them heels," he shook his head. "That red lipstick... you must want me to fuck that shit up."

Misani giggled and pecked his lips. "It doesn't go anywhere so you can try."

Nasty thoughts of her sucking his dick on the way to their destination flooded his mind and Misani already knew what he was thinking.

"Nope," she laughed, grabbing her YSL clutch from the dresser.

"I ain't even say anything," he proclaimed following her out the bedroom.

"You didn't have to. I saw the look in your eyes when you licked your lips."

He grinned behind her, loving the way the leather of her skirt hugged her ass, hips and waist. He'd already made plans in his mind to fuck her with those dollar sign pumps on and watch her come all over him. It was a must.

"I'm saying; let me test the product out and see how wet resistant it is."

Misani chortled loudly, stepping into his three-car garage. "Later on. I got you," she told him as he pulled the passenger door open for her.

"I know you do."

Headed to their destination, Misani texted her girls in a group chat letting them know it was time for their weekly lunch date. With everything going on in each of their lives, they'd been so busy and missed a few. Misani let them know she was out with her boo and of course Zari being Zari had to ask where she was going. It was out of habit more than being nosey, though.

"Bae, where we going again? You said a friend of yours is having an anniversary party, right?"

Carlo nodded. "Yeah. My boy Enzo and his fiancée Harlem are celebrating the one-year anniversary of their hookah lounge being opened. You smoke hookah?"

"Rarely, but I will today."

Carlo glanced her way and grabbed her hand just as his phone rang. Kissing her wrist, he let it go and answered his sister's call. Before when she used to blow his line down, Carlo would be annoyed knowing she didn't want anything. Now he'd tried getting to it the first couple times it rang if possible. Her kidnapping had fucked him up, but everyone involved had been dealt with. According to Xander at least. He wasn't letting Misani in on any of the details of what went down and for his own reasons. Some shit just didn't need to be said aloud or repeated.

"What up sis," he answered.

"Hey. Can you check and see if Monae left her backpack in your truck? She said her tablet is in there and it better be."

Staying faithful to his duties as an uncle, Carlo had taken Monae to school a few times during the week and picked her up. Marisa was still somewhat on the leery side of being out in public, and he understood that. With time, she'd get better though. He hoped she did. Prayed the incident didn't place a hold on her life.

Rotating in her seat, Misani looked in the backseat for her backpack and found it on the floor behind her. Lifting it, she placed it in her lap. She'd ridden with Carlo a few times in the afternoon to pick Monae up and the two were slowly building their relationship.

Monae had been slightly afraid of Misani at first and she couldn't blame her. To see the same woman who pulled her out of a closet dating her uncle was hard for her to grasp at first. Carlo had to sit her down and explain how Misani wasn't a bad person, she was just stuck in a bad situation. That seemed to make things better, but only when Misani started coming around did Monae fully begin to like her without judgment. She'd forever remember that night and thank her though.

"Yeah. I got it. I'll bring it by there right quick."

"You sure? She can wait until you're not busy. I know you have things to do," she said not wanting to be a burden.

"Sis, it's cool. Tell her I'm on the way."

"Okay," she sighed. "Thank you. For everything."

Carlo's chest tightened. "Always. You know I got you for life and after that."

In the passenger seat, Misani sat with a smile on her face. Carlo was such a good man. No, a great one, and she knew he'd make an amazing husband one day.

"Do you want to get married?" she asked and he chuckled softly.

"Yeah. Why you ask that? You wanna marry a nigga or something? Don't get down on one knee and get yo ass embarrassed."

She smacked his arm and laughed. "I would never. A man couldn't pay me to make a fool of myself like that. I was just asking in general, though."

Carlo had always thought getting married was some fly shit. His parents had exemplified what real black love looked, felt and should be like. A man who wasn't his biological father had raised Carlo into the strong-willed man he was today, and his mother coddled him just enough to let him know how women were supposed to be taken care of.

"Yeah, I do. I told you in Jamaica you were my wife; don't fake now," he smirked, placing a hand on her thigh.

When the chauffeur on their first vacation together mistook her for Mrs. Pryce, she tried to disagree but failed. In fact, her first name with his last had a ring to it. When they pulled into the gated community Carlo moved Marisa into, he nodded toward the security he hired to keep a watch over them. The last thing he needed was for Marisa to come up missing again or worse, Monae.

Once Marisa let her daughter know that her uncle was on the way, Monae sat in the foyer of their home, peeping out the window every minute. When she saw him pulling into the driveway, she hopped up and started to open the door but stopped. Looking over her shoulder, she waited for her mama to come into view. Marisa appreciated her listening skills and told her so.

"Thank you for being a big girl and listening. You can open it," she said kissing her forehead.

Monae damn near flung the door off the hinges and was down the steps before Carlo could get out. "Uncle Lo!" she shouted rushing toward him.

Carlo swooped her up, tossing her little body into the

air a few times. She wasn't the lightest child, but he made it seem like it. "What up my favorite girl in the world," he beamed.

She kissed his cheek. "Muah! Am I really?"

"Yep," he nodded. "But you're not going to be if you keep leaving this in my car. You have some important things in here and can't just be leaving it lying around anywhere okay?"

She pouted with her lip poked out but nodded. "Okay. Is that Mis-Mis," she stopped with furrowed brows. "I can't pronounce her name."

"Never say you can't do anything. It's just difficult to say. Let's go ask her so you can practice."

She grinned and rushed toward the passenger door when he put her down. Walking up to the house, Carlo gave his sister a once over. She looked much better than she had when she first came home, and he liked the short hairstyle she was now rocking. That was new to him.

"I like the cut," he told her as they hugged.

"Thank you. Letting go of dead weight, you know."

He nodded. "Fasho. Here's her bag. Y'all good? You need anything? How your pockets?"

Marisa chuckled. "I'm fine Carlo. You don't have to give me money every time you see me now. With Brook- with him out the picture now, I'm starting to have my own money again. Even started a nice little savings account for me and Monae."

Carlo was proud. "That's what's up. I'm proud of you. Rather you need something or not; I'ma always ask. You know that."

Marisa smiled. "I do. You're just like daddy. Did ma text you about family dinner tomorrow?"

"Yeah. Talking about I better bring the woman her grandbaby has been talking about."

They shared a laugh as Marisa watched Misani remove the earring from her ear and hold it up against Monae's. Her baby girl was a diva in the making and she loved it.

"Can I have them?" Monae asked looking into the visor mirror.

Misani chuckled. "No ma'am. These are too grown for you. If your mama lets me, I'll get you some smaller ones that are for your age okay?"

"Okay! I like you. My uncle likes you too."

"Does he?"

She nodded. "Mhm. He's never brought a woman friend around, so he must like you. Plus, you're pretty and have baby hairs like me so he has to like you."

Misani couldn't help but laugh. Monae was too much for her. "Well, thank you sweetie. You're pretty too. Do you like school?"

"Yes. I have a friend named Daiya in my class who has this crazy uncle who's really her cousin but calls him her uncle. I don't know why. It's kinda funny. She has a puppy. I'ma ask Uncle Lo to get me one for my birthday. It's so tiny though. Do you have a puppy?"

Struggling to keep up with the seven-year-old, Misani answered her question. "Nope. No pets. When's your birthday? I bet I can convince him to buy you one."

Monae gasped, mouth wide open. "Really!?"

"Mhm -umph," she let out as Monae threw her body into hers and hugged her tightly around the neck.

"Thank you! I knew you weren't mean."

Misani's eyes widened, taken aback by her choice of words but hugged her anyway. She meant no harm and she knew that. "You're welcome. Now, when's your birthday? It'll be our little secret, so don't tell him. I'll make him think it's for me."

"It's October twenty-sixth," she whispered just as Carlo pulled the driver's door open.

"Gotcha," Misani told her and smiled.

Carlo looked back and forth between them. "What y'all whispering about?"

"That's our business, sir. Ain't that right?" Misani asked Monae and she nodded with a big grin on her face. She couldn't wait for her and Daiya to have play dates with their puppies.

Carlo feigned hurt, holding a hand to his chest. "Like that Monae? I thought you were my favorite girl?"

"I am! Misani can be your favorite girl too, though. We have our own business."

He chuckled and shook his head. "A'ight. I see how it is. Come give me a hug so I can leave."

Monae hugged Misani one more time before running around to the front of the truck where Carlo met her. "I'll see you tomorrow at Granny's."

"Okay. Love you!" she shouted, rushing up the steps.

"Love you too."

Inside the truck, he backed out and pulled out of the community with his heart full. He had his doubts about Misani's place in his life, especially after that night, but seeing the way she made Monae's face light up and brought a calming to his life, he knew she was here to stay.

"I just love her little self," Misani told him.

"She's about to have you wrapped around her finger," Carlo said with a shake of his head.

"Like I have her uncle, huh?" she said leaning over and pecking the side of his mouth. Inhaling that masculine scent she could just bathe in if possible.

Running a hand down his thick, jet black waves that laid so perfectly, Carlo smirked, knowing she was telling nothing but the truth. "You already know."

CHAPTER EIGHT

Misani, Envie and Keegan all sat inside their favorite restaurant where they had their lunch dates, with their mouths wide open. Keegan had a smirk on her face while Misani giggled, trying to pull herself together. Envie was probably the only one who hadn't seen this coming. Not from Zari anyway.

"You said what?" Envie asked her.

"I think I'm pregnant," Zari whined and pushed her plate away from her.

"By who?" Keegan snickered.

"Who the hell else?" she hissed making them all laugh. "Stop laughing. I'm serious y'all. I've been super emotional and my period is nowhere in sight. Like the hoe playing hide and seek or something."

Misani chuckled, sipping her wine. "I know Flip is happy."

"That ain't the daddy," Keegan joked and Zari tossed a crouton at her head.

"Shut the fuck up; yes he is."

"I know. Calm down meanie. You two minutes pregnant and already on my nerves."

"You the one who jinxed me! You and Flip. Talking about a baby will sit my ass down somewhere. Now look at me," she huffed tossing her hands in the air.

Envie smiled. "It'll be fine. You're acting like you won't be an amazing mother. Plus, you have us to support you."

"Yeah and your dad. How are things with him going?" Misani asked.

"Surprisingly better than I thought. He's consistent as fuck," she groaned but softly smiled. "He's really taking this get to know me thing seriously."

"At least one of our parents are," Keegan said. No emotion was in her voice and they knew why.

After her night at Ramzi's, who was the perfect gentleman, she stuck to her word and let Chrissy's issues be just that; her own. It was nothing new, but it'd been weeks since she heard anything about her and Keegan was okay with that. She'd been focusing on her for once and it felt damn good. Her skin was glowing, sleep wasn't interrupted, relationship with Ramzi was flourishing and her bank account was increasing.

"That's good. It's a healthy relationship and you need that," Misani said chewing on her chicken and spinach panini.

"Now that Zari's good news is out, what else is going on?" Envie asked.

"I enrolled in school," Keegan announced, and they all started dancing.

"Ayyye. Okay, cousin! I'm happy for you," Envie grinned.

"Me too!" Misani and Zari added.

"Jinx you owe me a—" Zari started but got cut off.

"A what?" Misani laughed.

"A babysitter for life hoe."

They laughed and Keegan continued.

"Thanks y'all. I'm nervous, but it's a start. I need a fresh start and something that'll occupy my time."

"Once I have this baby, you'll be occupied alright," Zari grumbled.

"What're you thinking of majoring in?" Envie asked.

"Finance. As much money as we done touched, I need to start investing and start my own business."

Misani nodded her head. "Hell yes. I was thinking about that the other day. We know so many bosses; it's time to become our own."

"Exactly like your shirt says, 'Boss Babes Link Up'," Envie added.

Zari frowned. "That's what BBLU stands for? I thought it meant Boss Bitches."

"It could mean that, but Amiya and Maliya wanted to promote it differently. I got y'all one in the car once we leave here."

Misani had done a little shopping before their lunch date and stopped by her favorite clothing store *MAG. Co.* The owners were twin sisters in their twenties who had been in the fashion industry since teenagers and were making themselves known worldwide. Being an exclusive member, Misani was able to get her and her girls the limited edition *BBLU* tee. She was even thinking of a way to collaborate with them on a few things but had to figure out what first.

"I love them and their fine ass brother Sen," Zari said and Keegan tooted her lips out.

"A'ight. I thought you were done fucking on other women's men?"

"She couldn't fuck him if she tried," Misani laughed. "His wife does not play about that man."

"You know his wife?" Envie asked.

"No. I follow her on social media though and she be checking the fuck out of women who get beside themselves in the comments under her pictures of him."

Zari smiled. "Umm. I need to go lurk his Instagram."

"You are messy," Keegan laughed. "Don't get beat up."

"I ain't lost a fight a day in my life. Don't play with me."

"Blah, blah. What else is new? Oh, wait!" Misani screeched then giggled. The wine she was sipping had her feeling good.

"Lush ass," Zari snickered.

"Whatever. Envie, I didn't get all the details about your baby daddy coming home. Me and Zari were talking about it, but she never called me back."

"Y'all stay running y'all mouth about me," Envie said, rolling her eyes playfully.

"We can do that cause we love you. I was just telling her how big your eyes got when you saw him," Zari chuckled. "Bet that lil' pussy got wet too, huh?"

Envie mushed her in the arm. "Shut up. But y'all, on the real that nigga went to jail and got fine as ever."

"Aaaah," Misani laughed. "You want that old thang back, huh?"

Envie's upper lip turned up. "Never. Fine or not, that man belongs to the streets and always has. Y'all should've seen all the screenshots Elise sent me of girls welcoming him home. I don't want anything to do with him."

"Nah, you only saying that cause Urban been laying

that NBA dick off in you like a slam dunk contest," Zari told her.

"A slam dunk?" Keegan giggled.

"Mhm, real forceful. Balls deep in her little ass," she laughed. "Y'all should've seen the way she was walking."

"You should've recorded her!" Misani laughed.

"Y'all really get on my nerves. I like him and there isn't a thing Zaire could do to make me fool with him again. His only option is to be there for Azai," she told them. "Misani, you can't talk. You've been over Carlo's house playing auntie with his niece."

She rolled her eyes. "That's my girl. She invited me to her school to have lunch with her and I didn't know what to say y'all."

"You better go support that baby," Envie replied.

"I want to, but I'd feel so awkward. Her mama doesn't like getting out of the house at all. Even with Carlo having security with them. It's so sad."

The closer she and Carlo became, the more she was around his family. Misani had finally met his parents and some of his other family members. A few fell in love with her instantly, especially his parents, while others were a little hesitant. That was only because Monae had run her mouth about who she was, but Carlo didn't care how they felt. They weren't the ones in a relationship with her or paying her bills.

"Being snatched up and held against your will is no joke," Keegan spoke lowly. "I still get paranoid some days."

"It'll get better, boo," Zari told her.

"I'll probably go. She kept telling me about one of her friends from the class who has a crazy cousin and I realized it was Sen. I had to put two and two together."

Misani had been scrolling her Instagram feed one day while Monae was next to her and Daiya and Sen's wife Neicey had posted a video. When she realized Daiya was the little girl Monae wanted a dog like, she then knew that Sen was the crazy cousin/uncle she'd told Monae about.

"Let me know when it is so I can go with you," Zari smirked just as Keegan's phone vibrated against the table. An unknown number popped up on the screen.

"I'ma tell Flip," she joked before answering the call. "Hello?"

"Hi. Is this Keegan Cole?"

Her brows dipped. "Yes, this is she. Who is this?"

"Oh, hi. My name is Monese. I'm calling from Fresh Start."

Keegan paused for a beat then said, "Okay... I'm not sure what business that is."

"We're a rehabilitation center in Kansas. Your mother, Chrissy, gave us your number to call."

Her heart sank. "Is she okay?" she said above a whisper.

Envie mouthed 'what's wrong?' but Keegan couldn't reply. She was too tuned in to what the woman was about to say. She held her breath, waiting for the bad news.

"Oh, yes. She's doing great actually. They aren't allowed to make phone calls for the first three weeks that they're here and she'd reached her three-week mark. I only called because she said hearing your voice would be a trigger and she's trying to stay strong."

Keegan choked on a cry and her eyes filled to the brim with tears. She had absolutely no idea that Chrissy had checked into rehab. Not just that, but she'd been in there for three weeks. That was a huge accomplishment from the couple of days she used to do then leave. Overwhelmed, Keegan cleared her throat.

"Wow. I'm surprised. Sorry if I sound a bit confused, but I had no idea she was there. Am I her emergency contact person?"

"Yes ma'am, you are."

"I don't know if you can tell me this but did someone force her to be there? Like, did someone help check her in?"

"She wasn't forced. Someone did help her check-in, but they asked to remain anonymous. I can send you over all her paperwork if you'd like."

"No. That's okay," she had to remind herself to look out for Keegan. "How long is the program she's in?"

"It's a ninety-day program and if passed successfully, there's a graduation once completing."

Keegan nodded. She could go ninety days without talking to her. She'd already planned in her mind that she'd go the rest of her life if that's what Chrissy wanted.

"Okay. That's not bad. I don't want any of the paperwork until she completes the program. I'm glad she's in there and I hope she stays. Can you tell her one thing for me though?"

"I sure can."

"Tell she's living her life and it's time I live mine. I'll see her when her ninety days are up at graduation."

Monese smiled. "I'll let her know, Ms. Cole. It was nice talking to you."

"You as well. Oh, wait. One more thing. Was this program covered through her insurance or how do the payments go?"

"Oh, it was paid for in full."

Her jaw dropped. "Seriously? What if she doesn't stay and how much was that?"

Monese chuckled. "Per the anonymous payer, I can't reveal the amount. If she doesn't stay, only the money spent while here will be charged plus a fee for leaving.

Addiction is a lifelong journey, but I have faith in your mother."

"Well that's good because I stopped long ago. Hopefully, she makes you and whoever she's doing this for proud. Thank you. Still, relay my message to her."

"I will. Have a good day."

"You too," Keegan replied before hanging up.

The table was quiet, not sure what to say after overhearing a conversation like that. Keegan was stunned. Chrissy was trying to turn over a new leaf, but Keegan wasn't holding her breath. She'd placed faith in her hundreds of times before and had been failed. Until she completed the program, Keegan didn't have anything to say.

"Someone paid for her to go to rehab?" Envie asked. It was her auntie so she wanted to know the details.

Keegan shoved some salad into her mouth and shrugged. "I guess so."

"You're not happy about it?" Misani wanted to know. "Seems like she's trying."

"It's not that I'm not happy. It's just that I broke my own heart looking out for her, expecting her to do the same in return and I'm not doing it again. I refuse."

Envie nodded, knowing exactly what she meant. She'd been there with Lenae one too many times.

"Who do you think paid a bill like that?" Zari asked.

"I have an idea who, but I'm not going to mention it. It was a sweet gesture and I want it to remain that way."

Misani smiled. "You think he did it looking for something in return?"

"I *know* he didn't do it for that reason. He fucks with me and wants to see me happy. That's the only reason."

Zari stretched her hand out so Keegan could give her a high-five. "I heard that. That man fucks with Kee the long way, baby. Tell him to pay my credit card off while he over there being generous."

"Hell, I got a light bill due right now," Envie added.

"You need something paid Misani?" Zari asked and Keegan shook her head with a grin.

Misani nodded and smiled. "Sure do. What he trying to pay, friend?"

Keegan smiled at her girls, thankful as hell for them. Honestly, she wouldn't know where she'd be in life had Misani not helped her out that day in Target. They'd been inseparable since. Back in the day, Keegan used to believe money was the root of all evil; but now it was starting to look like it had done them some good.

She was going to thank Ramzi for what he did, but only after Chrissy walked that stage. Yeah, he had money to spend to make Keegan happy, but Chrissy had to prove she was receiving help because she genuinely wanted to, not because Keegan wanted her to. Drinking from her wine glass, Keegan reminded herself to mark her calendar for the ninety-day mark. It'd be a day she'd never forget if Chrissy pulled through.

$$$

"Azai!" Envie yelled up the steps. "Your daddy will be here any minute. Get off that game and come put your shoes on."

"Ok!" he shouted and Envie shook her head.

She'd been fighting with him all morning about getting dressed so he wouldn't be rushing once Zaire showed up. He was picking him up for one of Azai's cousins on his side birthday party. Envie loved her child, but he'd been driving her up a wall since he'd gotten out of school yesterday evening.

Knowing his dad was coming to get him, Azai had been on ten. He and Zaire's relationship since he'd been released was what Envie prayed for. Azai had no reservations when it came to his dad and you better believe he was asking as many questions as possible. Envie found herself apologizing to Zaire for all of their son's questions, but he waved her off. Azai could ask him whatever he wanted because Zaire knew his little man needed an explanation from him. Not only as his father but as a man.

He may have not done a lot of things right in his life,

but he was damn sure going to give his all to being a father to his kids. That was one of the reasons Envie wanted Azai ready when he pulled up. He was showing effort with their co-parenting, and she didn't want to slack off. He was meeting her more than half-way and not out of guilt anymore.

"Mama, is he here?" Azai asked, rushing inside the kitchen.

Envie looked at her handsome son and grinned. He was getting so tall but still skinny as ever. She was letting his hair grow out some and his tendrils were popping. He looked just like his daddy and Envie knew it. The older he got, the more he looked like him.

"Not yet, but still put your shoes on. Did you bring your bag down?"

He shook his head and rushed back out. "I'll go get it."

"Stop running!" she said for what felt like the millionth time today.

Picking her phone up, she dialed her boo Urban and waited for him to answer. They had plans of their own once Azai was gone and Envie needed to change them. Not by much, but she was in need of some sex before they went anywhere and did anything.

"I'm still coming," he said once answering.

"That's exactly what I need to do," she whispered and he chuckled.

"Yeah? You already know I'ma handle that soon as I walk in the door."

Her eyes fluttered, imagining his head buried between her legs. "Mmm," she purred. "How far are you?"

"Give me five minutes. I want you naked and bent over too since you asking questions," he told her.

"Babe, Azai is still here," she giggled. "I'm waiting on his daddy."

"Even better. I get to meet the man who gave my wife a baby first."

Envie blushed. "Your wife? You're thinking mighty far ahead, aren't you?"

"I was always told the best way to plan your future, is to speak things into existence."

"Hmm. I like that. Just don't be speaking no babies into our future any time soon."

"Oh nah. Between yours and mine, we got a good year until I knock you up."

Envie snorted as the doorbell rang. "A year? Oh, hell nah. It better be a ring on my finger first."

"You can have it whatever way you want, beautiful. Either way, I'm dropping this dick off in you so gon' flirt with your baby daddy."

"Oh, hush," she giggled. "I'll see you when you get here."

"A'ight."

Hanging up, she pulled the door open to a cheesing Zaire. "What up? That's how you answer the door for me?"

Eyeing her body in the light blue shorts and tank top she was wearing, Zaire licked his lips and tried stepping inside. Envie chuckled and held her hand out.

"Un, un. You can stay right here. It's not too hot to wait outside. And, I wear what I want in my house."

"Yeah, a'ight. You don't gotta front for me. Turn around right quick though. I'm tryna see something," he smirked.

"Boy. Go to hell," she laughed just as Azai ran up with his shoes on and backpack in his hand.

"Mama, I can't find my iPad."

"It's in my room on the charger, but you don't need it. You're going to a birthday party," she reminded him, fixing the collar of his shirt.

"Daddy, do I need my iPad?"

Zaire looked at Envie, and she playfully rolled her eyes. Of course, he had to ask his daddy.

"Nope. We going somewhere where you won't even be thinking about it," he told him.

"Okay. Hey! There's Urban," he shouted, pushing past Zaire.

"You better not run down them steps," Envie scolded.

Turning in the direction his son was looking, Zaire

looked on as Urban pulled his heavily tinted Chevy Tahoe into the extra parking spot in her driveway. He heard that Envie was messing around with a ballplayer but didn't mention it to her. He knew her, and if she wanted to let him in on her love life she would. Zaire guessed today was that day.

"An NBA player, huh?" he asked looking her way. "I didn't have a chance, did I?"

"Not at all homeboy," she chuckled, watching Urban and Azai speak to one another in person for the first time. They'd talked on FaceTime plenty when Azai was laid up in Envie's bed or when she was talking to him around the house.

"That's fucked up. I guess I approve if he treating you and my youngin' right. He is treating y'all good, right?"

"Great actually," Envie smiled, genuinely letting him know exactly what was up. She didn't need his approval. Things between them were a for sure wrap.

Zaire nodded. "That's all that matter then. Let me go check this nigga right quick," he joked.

"Please grow up. Don't let him have a bunch of candy either. Oh, and not too much running."

"Envie, I got it. He's my child too. We good E; I promise. No need to worry when he's with me."

She sighed trying to calm her nerves. The first time they went out, she went with them so Azai could feel comfortable. The second time she let them go alone and cried almost the entire time. Now, she was shooing him out the door but still had her worries. Azai was her baby and after the shit her mama and Misha pulled, she was always going to be cautious. Zaire didn't play about his kids though. He got Misha's messy ass together quick when he touched down. All that mouth she had before ceased.

"Okay. Have him call me later," she told him.

"I will."

"Bye Mama!" Azai yelled, tugging on the passenger door his booster seat was in. Envie didn't care how tall he'd gotten; his weight still required him to be in a booster seat and he would be until he no longer had to.

"Come give me a hug little boy."

Envie didn't worry about what Zaire and Urban were discussing. Yes, Zaire could be childish from time to time, but he would never come out of his mouth and disrespect Envie. Urban wouldn't let him either. Placing a kiss to Azai's cheek, she hugged him tight just as Urban and Zaire dapped fists.

"I'll see you later. Have fun okay?"

"Okay, Mama. Bye Urban!"

He smirked. "Catch you later, dude."

After helping him get strapped in, Zaire backed out of the driveway and left. Urban couldn't even make it inside the house completely before Envie was jumping in his arms trying to remove his shirt. With her arms wrapped around his neck and legs around his waist, Urban palmed her booty and gave the right cheek a firm smack.

"I saw you flirting with him."

She giggled. "Babe, no I was not."

"That ain't what I saw. I think you need to be punished for that."

Her kitty purred the instant she did. "Mmm. You think so? I like a little punishment."

Scooting her shorts and panties to the side, Urban slid his hand across her slick slit. She was super wet for him already. Kissing him, Envie grinded on his hand until he was pushing his fingers inside her. She could deal with the foreplay for now, but she was going to need that dick in a minute.

Working his fingers, he whispered against her lips, "That pussy gushing already; I feel it."

That quickly, she was about to come. Envie's stomach tightened and her head fell lazily into the crook of his neck. She came fast and hard. Legs shaking, Urban toyed with her clit making her first orgasm of the evening that much better.

Envie kissed along his neck and breathed hard. "Damn, babe."

Urban slid his hands from inside her shorts and licked his fingers. "That pussy been marinating all day, huh?"

She cackled at his observation. "It's only noon. Quit playing."

"Shit. I'm just saying. You taste so fucking good," he growled.

Envie licked her lips. "Let me see."

With no hesitation, Urban slipped her his tongue and walked them toward her bedroom while they lip-locked. Just as bad as she wanted him, he wanted her too. Placing her on the bed, he removed his shirt. Running her hands along his eight-pack, she shivered at his body. It was seriously the sexiest body she'd seen and was proud to claim him as hers.

"I'm glad you and Zaire met today," she told him, running her dainty size four foot along the imprint of his dick.

Urban pulled his shorts and his boxers down for her. His erection popped out like a jack-in-the-box. "Yeah? Why's that?"

"Because," she said lowly, crawling toward the edge of the bed. "Now I don't have to lie about where I'm at when he calls for Azai."

He smirked. "So you been lying huh? Ain't wanna tell this man who I was?"

"What? No. That's not it. I just – Urban!" she laughed as he began to tickle her.

Falling onto her side, Envie tried moving away from him, but he pinned himself atop her. Leaving her no place to go, Urban flipped her onto her back and held her arms above her head with her wrists enclosed in one of his hands.

"You know how ticklish I am. I will be pee on myself for real," she told him, trying to hold her laughs back and be serious.

"I ain't into the kinky shit, so I'ma stop," he chuckled. "On the real, I'm glad we met too. Did that make you happy to get it over with?"

She nodded her head. "Yeah. I knew Azai would tell him sooner or later. He likes you."

"Good, cause I love his mama and she gon' have my last name and a baby in her by next year."

Envie's eyes softened and pussy got wetter. "That's a bet?"

"That's a promise," he smirked, covering her hardened nipple with his thick lips and even thicker tongue.

Envie moaned softly. "I love you too."

"I already knew that," he said cockily lifting up. "Now spread them legs for me. It's time to pay up."

Happily, Envie let him remove her shorts and panties before he slid so deeply inside her, her eyes crossed. She told not one lie when admitting to loving him because it was the truth. What was meant to be a one-night stand to hit a lick, had turned into Envie finding her true happiness. She made a mental reminder to thank Zari and her scheming ass for 'setting' him up. Urban was hers to keep now; no givebacks.

CHAPTER NINE

6 MONTHS LATER

"Would you like to know the gender of your baby?" Zari's doctor, Dr. Neuf, asked.

Smiling, Zari glanced over at Flip who was staring intently at the ultrasound screen. He had a serious expression on his face, but that was how he always looked when they visited. Trying to decipher what part of his child's body was what, he remained focused. This was both their first child and he needed every question answered.

"Alphonso," Zari tittered with laughter in her voice. "The baby isn't moving anywhere from that screen."

"It might," he offered sitting back. "My fault Doc; what'd you ask?"

Dr. Neuf smiled. She loved first-time parents and

their excitement. "Do you both want to know the gender or are we keeping it a secret?"

"I want to know," Zari offered. "I've been waiting long enough."

"It's whatever she wants," Flip told her and meant it.

Whatever Zari wanted, he wouldn't hesitate to get. Except for those damn boiled eggs with hot sauce and ranch that she craved in the wee hours of the morning. He almost tossed all the eggs in the trash but knew he'd get cursed smooth out. Zari's farts had been vicious and damn near made Flip pass out.

"Okay. Let's see then," she said moving the probe covered in gel along her belly. "Here's the leg and if it just moves a bit... you'll see his penis," she smiled. "You're having a boy. Congratulations!"

Zari's eyes watered as Flip stood to his feet to hug her. "Thank goodness," she whispered and kissed his lips.

Triumph soared through Flip's chest. He would be happy with either gender, but he was elated to know he'd be getting his boy first. The way Zari had been acting, in such a good mood her entire pregnancy once the second trimester hit, Flip had no doubt in his mind that he'd be knocking her up again right after their son was born. He wanted to keep her ass sitting down for a while. The hot girl in her still resided; that he knew.

"Thank you, ma," he told her, rubbing her round

belly.

"You're welcome. Can we go eat now?"

Dr. Neuf chuckled as she wiped the gel from Zari's belly. "You're free to go. I'll see you during your next visit Ms. Byrd. Congratulations again."

"Thanks so much."

When Dr. Neuf left out of the room, Flip helped Zari down from the table and gave her a real hug. Their son was active as ever and kicking his daddy in the stomach.

"Yeah, he protective of you already. Cockblocking in the womb."

Zari chuckled. "Hush. He's hungry shoot. I can't wait to call Misani and the girls. She's going to be so upset."

"Why? She wanted you to have a girl?"

"Mhm. We all did. Well, I didn't care honestly. I'm just glad he's healthy."

Flip nodded and opened the door for her. "Me too. That's what matters. Plus, I didn't need my baby girl influenced by all you women in the family."

"Oh please. As if we'd steer her wrong."

Flip stopped walking and looked at her with a blank stare. "Do you not see how you turned out?"

Snatching her hand from his, Zari flipped him off. She didn't care about them being in the doctor's office at all. "I turned out amazing, sweetie. You wouldn't be here if I hadn't."

Laughing, Flip grabbed ahold of her hand again. "On the real I think you trapped me; you know how you do."

"I'm sick of you and these slick jokes. Come on and feed me before I snap on your ass," she hissed and he rubbed her belly while waiting on the elevator.

"There she goes. I was waiting for the real you to come out. Give me a kiss."

Zari stayed facing forward with a smile on her face. "Nope."

Gently, Flip grabbed her chin and looked down in her eyes. He loved him some Zariella and she knew it. He was wrapped around her finger and wasn't letting loose anytime soon. He smooched her lips just as the elevator door opened.

"I love you."

Zari's stomach and heart fluttered. "I love you too, baby. For real. I'm so glad I didn't make you a lick back when we first met."

Flip cocked his head back. "Yo, what?"

She laughed. "Yes, trust me, you were going to be one until you told me about myself that night in your car. That's when I knew you were different. I told Jhalil I wasn't gon' do you like that and now look. Got a whole baby in my damn belly. Ain't this some shit."

Flip didn't even know what to say. Zari was so unpredictable, he rolled with whatever she was doing most days.

As her man he knew this, but as a man he still had a say so. They'd both gotten to a place in their relationship where Zari no longer shut down when he said something she didn't want to hear, and Flip gave her space to come to terms with what he was asking of her and vice versa.

The relationship blossoming between her and Zeek was a part of her and Flip's relationship growth as well. Zeek was very active in her life now and let it be known. His family had some slick shit to say about it, but he checked them and whoever. Zari had to come to terms with realizing people made mistakes. Not everyone was perfect regardless of how life and social media made them seem. She forgave her father and thanked God every day her child had a father who would be in his life. She knew that for a fact.

Keegan had been on the same forgiveness wave as Zari. Sticking to her word, Keegan didn't contact or see her mother until she crossed the stage at her graduation. She looked healthier and cleaner than she'd ever seen her. Keegan had let her hurt go and was trying to build with Chrissy, but no less than two months after she'd passed the program, she had relapsed.

In true Chrissy fashion, she went missing for weeks at a time. Keegan no longer felt guilty for her drug addiction. She'd done all she could and given so much of her life up to her mother who in return just slapped her in the face.

With her focus now solely on school, Keegan could only hope and pray that God kept Chrissy covered because she no longer could. Sometimes, you just can't save them all and she learned that.

In the car, Zari dialed up Misani while Flip drove to a Chipotle nearby since she wanted a chicken bowl. Living her best life, Misani stood in the sun as it began to set in Mykonos Greece. The private villa had the most amazing view that came equipped with its own cave, calmness and ambiance Misani cherished. So much of her life had been on the go, she'd taken the time over the last two months to travel the world.

Zari was going to have to call her back. Her phone was tucked away inside the villa, having had already taken enough pictures since they arrived. She wanted to enjoy the moment. Wanted to thank God for allowing her to experience what she was without any distractions.

Walking up behind her, Carlo admired her beauty from afar. Her golden butter pecan skin was glowing, making him slowly drag his tongue over his lips. Hair blowing in the breeze, free from the bun she'd had it in. Her striking yet humble beauty is was what attracted him to her to begin with. When he grew to know the selfless her, the woman who'd put her life on the line for her own, the her who made money in her sleep, challenged him to think deeper, love stronger and try harder... Carlo knew she was it for him. She was honestly his equal.

"I know you're enjoying the view," she teased without facing him.

Carlo smirked. Placing himself behind her, loving the softness of her plump ass in the thong swimsuit she had on, he kissed the spot directly behind her right ear.

"I was until you interrupted me. What you out here thinking about?"

Misani sighed. "Just life. How grateful I am for having made it this far. I've been through so much."

"You have, but you overcame that shit like the boss you are. You deserve this right here, ma. Know that."

"I do, and these trips have had me thinking about what I want to do when I get back home. I have to do more. Feel more. Live more. Be more than what I am now."

Nodding, Carlo moved to the side of her. "I like the sound of that. You're motivating me," he chuckled.

"Remember that night in Jamaica you explained to me what the tattoo's on your hands mean?" she asked him.

"Yeah. You thinking about getting some more ink?"

"Not yet. It's just what you said has stuck with me. It's engraved into my mind every time I think of my life. I'm reminded to love my life. The people in it, what it's done and taken from me, where it's leading me and all. I love you for sharing that; it changed my mindset for good," she said, getting a bit emotional.

Carlo tossed his arms around her shoulder and pulled her into his side. Kissing her temple, he let his lips linger there. "You have an open mind and that's what I love the most about you. Your heart is so pure, ma. Whatever you do in this world, wherever you leave your mark, it'll be more than appreciated and remembered. I can promise you that."

She blushed and wrapped her arm around his waist. "Thank you. Where do you want to travel to next?"

"It doesn't matter. As long as we're living it up and will enjoy it, you can choose."

"Good. Because I already picked it," she laughed as he swooped her up. "D'Carlo!" she shouted as he jumped in the pool of their private villa.

When they came from under, Misani was shaking her head while he had a smirk on his face.

"Don't look like that, acting like you can't get wet."

She smirked. "Oh, you and I both know how wet I can get."

Carlo swam towards her in two quick strokes and had her pinned against the white wall. Lifting her up, he moved her thong out the way and pulled his dick from his swim trunks. Already rocked up, he slid inside her, loving the way her sexy ass eyes flickered with pleasure.

"Shit," he groaned, pumping into her. "You are wet."

"I told you. Make me come before the sun disappears," she moaned.

With one mission to complete, bringing her to her peak, Carlo did just that. If anyone told Misani ten years ago that she'd be making love in her favorite vacation spot to date, to the love of her life, with not a care in the world, she'd pay them the loose change she didn't have to stop lying.

So much had changed since the seventeen-year-old her fled the group home. Life had matured her quicker than she'd expected it to, but she wouldn't have had it any other way. Her life lessons were meant to be taught and experienced. With a massive payout from Xander, once she retired from the cleaning services, Misani saved it all.

She knew what it was like to be dead broke and struggling for her next meal and place to sleep and never wanted to experience that again. When she got home, she was looking into opening up a girl's home or some type of program that would teach them life skills. Empower women to be their best selves even when the world wanted them to conform and was against them. Misani, Zari, Envie and Keegan had all learned to survive through their obstacles by winging it and leaning on one another. They didn't have a mentor or women in their life who assisted them.

Surviving the hell they went through wasn't about just living through it, but to actually live. Not for anyone else, but for themselves. That was another reason why Misani had gone on vacation. She needed time to herself. She would've hated to die and had not lived, because there was so much more to life than death. So much more than the money that had almost taken them out. More than being motherless or fatherless daughters. More than being the go-to for everyone who needed her.

The money hadn't changed them. It gave them a better understanding of what it could do if they'd let it. At the end of the day, money can't buy you happiness or erase your pain. It can't buy you love or the type of friendship they shared. Not the genuine kind anyway.

On their mission to survive, receive love, embrace self-love, grasp what it meant to be understanding, seek patience, overcome abandonment and no longer beg for acceptance; these girls had beat all odds against them and stacked their money to live a life they'd almost lost to obtain. They now realized that girls didn't just wanna have funds; they wanted solid friendships and love too. Thankfully, they were each awarded the desires of their heart...even though it'd taken a while to receive.

The End.

ACKNOWLEDGMENTS

Thank you so much for reading! I hope you enjoyed Misani, Zari, Keegan, and Envie's story.
To my readers, thanks for rocking with me! Part 2 took much longer to write than planned, but y'all were patient and I appreciate that SO MUCH!

To stay up to date with releases and all things concerning my books, ***subscribe to my email list.*** Also, join my reading group on Facebook! **Be sure to answer the questions to gain access!**
BOOKS & BEYOND

For your chance to WIN $100 or a signed paperback copy of GJWHF series, send a

screenshot of your review to my email brianndanaebooks@gmail.com by November 2nd! There will be TWO winners! Good luck!

OTHER BOOKS BY ME

If you enjoyed this series, don't hesitate to snag a few more... or all of my other books. Here's some I'd recommend you start with.

He's Your Ex For A Reason
She From The Gutta 1-2
Juvie & Solai: A Hood Love Story 1-4
When She's Broken
Am I Good Enough To Love
Feenin' For A G 1-2
In No Need For Love 1-2
She Used To Be The Sweetest Girl
He Want That Old Thang Back

ABOUT THE AUTHOR

BriAnn Danae

AUTHOR

A lover of everything romance and what it entails, BriAnn beautifully merges complex urban socio-economic realities into her writing, and presents her novels in a way her readers can relate. Though fictional, she grasps the attention of her audience, snatches their breath away with each page, and leaves them yearning for more by the end of the book.

A lasting impression of her work, is what BriAnn strives to leave behind once the readers close out the pages. The Urban Romance genre - as she calls it - isn't just butterflies in your stomach, or dark and gritty, as describe by the internet. She classifies her writing as soul snatching, heart yearning, chest throbbing, and downright some of the most exhilarating literature one could grace their eyes upon.

CPSIA information can be obtained
at www.ICGtesting.com
Printed in the USA
LVHW022347220721
693426LV00011B/758